PARK WEST

A Novel of Love and Murder and Redemption

STANLEY GOLDSTEIN

PARK WEST

A Novel of Love and Murder and Redemption

WYSTON BOOKS, INC.

WYSTON BOOKS, INC.
P.O. Box 1280
Warwick, NY 10990-1280

Tel.: (845) 986-6888
E-mail: *wystonbooks@gmail.com*
Please visit our Website: *www.wystonbooks.com*

This is a work of fiction. Names, characters, places and incidents are the product of the author's imagination or used fictitiously. Any resemblance to actual events, locations, or persons, living or dead, is coincidental.

Publisher's Cataloging-in-Publication Data
Goldstein, Stanley
Park West: A Novel of Love and Murder and Redemption/
Stanley Goldstein—1st ed.
Includes bibliography
1. Psychiatry—Fiction
2. Clergy Life & Duties—Fiction
3. Military Life—Fiction

Library of Congress Control Number: 2002108492
813'.54—dc20
Cover photograph by Martin Barraud/OJO Images
Licensed from Getty Images

ISBN: 978-0-9717705-4-6 (print edition)
ISBN: 978-0-9717705-7-7 (E-book edition)

...for the lord knows the way of the righteous,
but the way of the wicked will perish.

—Psalms 1

CONTENTS

x

FOREWORD

DARLINGS,

I may be dead when you read this. Possibly your mother too. I wanted it this way, feeling that some events were too personal to share while we lived and are still dangerous for you to know. As you might expect *she* objected, so the final decision will be hers.

I began writing this record as salvation. Later, after I gained answers, it became a story. Then, finally, just a life.

And like all lives it's fragmented, created from memories long gone. Except our love for you—always...

PREFACE

I NEVER LIKED lawyers: they charge too much, don't return phone calls, and have business practices which would cause the suspension of my medical license yet are ignored by their peers. So after my arrest I feared that mine would behave in these ways.

"What should we handle first?" I asked her. "New York wants my medical license, the government froze my assets, and the Manhattan prosecutor is deciding whether he can arrange for my lethal injection more quickly than Texas or to let Alabama electrocute me."

"Think, don't obsess," a psychoanalyst told me long ago. This being expanded on by my lawyer who advised me to "try to find some pattern in the events—prosecutors can be wrong or even criminal but are never stupid."

So I now follow her advice and analyze my life believing, as I've told patients, that the unconscious knows what is crucial and will spontaneously raise it to awareness for deliberation. But I also knew that the unconscious had no sense of time and I was running out of time.

CHAPTER ONE

Long after I left medical school I took a course in sex feeling it was time I knew something about it. That's how I tell this story but it really concerned sexual development and was taught by a well-known OB-GYN who was also (and this is unusual) a very human guy. He began the first class by answering a silly question as to how he related to all the naked women he saw by saying that a doctor should react to *all* vulvae as if they were the same though (and he said this with a small smile) some *are* prettier than others.

But it was his later story which I cherish. A lonely woman, after meeting a man through a personal ad, invited him to her apartment where she was beaten and raped. When she berated her stupidity this doctor said, simply, "lonely people sometimes do unwise things." I often remembered these words and felt better, even as I tried to avoid doing them.

Freud stressed that personal involvement by a doctor was contrary to the patient's welfare. But I always felt involved. So maybe my troubles really began when I opened my practice...on Central Park West...

You can find apartment houses like mine all over the upper west side of New York City. Swarming with therapists of varying academic degree, theoretical persuasion, and ethics, these ornately carved buildings seem separate from the pace and worries of the collective City.

Their lobbies are quiet and on cloudy days a gloom emanates from the phony, heavily carved medieval style furniture and bogus "antique" rugs in the lobby, these seeming an extension of the artifice strewn structure of the therapy session itself.

People believe that psychiatrists must like their patients but I didn't like the Reverend Cary McMasterby, Doctor of Divinity: his pomposity and arrogance were almost too much to bear. But protected by my self-control and professional facade, I asked during one therapy session the only question which then came to mind.

"Why did you do it?"

"She needed me," he said.

I made my frequent mental note that "needy" women abused by clergymen are usually young and pretty.

"When did it start?" I asked.

"That's difficult to say," he responded, after gazing at the Rorschach-like abstract above my head, then the clouds and off-white painted door. Finally, as if having gained profound insight from these views, he spoke slowly and deliberately. His manner and deep voice impressed even me who knew that his response would be, invariably, bullshit.

6

"Did my sin begin when I touched her? Or when I vowed to help her as she worked while her husband drank, struggling to raise their children. Then I did comfort her. But first only as a Christian. This can be difficult to understand without the proper upbringing."

Reverend Cary was alluding to my being Jewish and being as tactful as usual. I knew what he *wanted* to say. I've sometimes wondered how I came to be considered expert at treating sexually abusing Christian clergymen. Catholic or Protestant, they're referred to me.

Rabbis never come. With them I don't have the *in*; gentiles are most comfortable that I'm *out* though religion has little to do with their troubles. Which can happen when lonely people become driven by unconscious motives and the power of authority and symbol.

Some clergy want their lives to become unmuddled. Most, just my letter stating that they completed treatment and are unlikely to act-out again. Or whatever phrases are needed for them to get on with their careers.

It was Cary's fourth session and I still didn't feel as if I knew him—which meant that he was one very guarded guy indeed. Cary was angry at his wife and again refused my suggestion that I interview her. Maybe being afraid that I would reveal how many women he provided "Christian warmth" to despite my assurance that what he told me was confidential. Or possibly he feared giving information which would conflict with his impressive facade. Or was in a bad mood and rejecting every request that day.

I was tired and so was Cary's therapy but we played our roles. He had sexually seduced women and was now psychologically seducing me as his persistent mellifluous voice described the Episcopal religion's ability to satisfy my yearning for greater belonging, though my faith had preceded his by several thousand years.

Like every tempter he sensed what I most wanted to hear and promised its fulfillment: in exchange for my statement that he wasn't really that bad. He had spoken and spoken and I knew him no better but he felt relieved: believing that he convinced me of his goodness; feeling less stress (which is what happens in psychotherapy); mostly, just being glad that his session was nearly over.

I said my usual, "We're going to have to stop now." As was usual, he stood, nodded, and left the office—silently. Had he responded, "with God's grace," which was my continuous fantasy, I couldn't have taken it. But that day he made one more statement.

"I'm sensing that the greatest spiritual grace can be gained from helping children."

The day dragged on. Early mornings I treated adults before they left for jobs on Madison Avenue and Wall Street. Then mothers, more relaxed with their older children in school, and freer to confront their crumbling marriages.

In the afternoons the children arrived. First the youngest, with those attending regular school after three. At six the adults returned and my energy became renewed from no longer having to play Chutes and Ladders and my work day being nearly over.

I was worn out.

Twenty years of worry had taken its toll. Thousands of experiences of caring deeply, then never seeing the patient again—which I knew was my job—had wiped me out. Their lives got better; mine didn't. I was "a rock for patients" (as an insurance executive once described me) but had myself become hardened and unable to change.

Until—as if from some unknown symmetry—one work day ended as it began. With another intriguing patient I didn't like who phoned, apparently, only because he had never heard of me.

"D'ya know my name? It's often in the papers," he asked in his initial call.

"No," I responded.

I stopped reading newspapers long before moving back to New York City from my many temporary jobs across America. While working for the government years before, I had at first-hand learned of the lies which were used to explain public events and so no longer believed uninformed uproar. Thereafter, seeking to relax and shield myself from these matters, I collected antique pistols, wandered through stores seeking toys for my office, and baked fat-free chocolate cakes which made me popular with neighbors: being continually obsessed with my ten pounds overweight I gave all away.

Which was why I had never heard of The General. Some days, when I was worried about a patient, I never noticed the sky. Even I regarded this as unhealthy.

"I'll pay cash. I won't use my insurance," he later added.

"Why not? You're paying for it."

"I don't want any records kept."

He demanded this as a pen and pad lay on a clipboard in my lap. I kept *extensive* notes for they had once having saved my career when I became embroiled in a lawsuit between an erotically disturbed woman and her equally intense husband.

"I have to keep them. But they're locked in a cabinet and I do everything including the typing and cleaning the office. If I don't file an insurance claim, nothing is sent out."

"*Everything* is confidential?"

"Within limits. I have to report if you're abusing a child, or a judge orders me to testify.

"What if I'm thinking of killing someone?"

"Only if the plan is realistic and you're not using a figure of speech. You get arrested for real murder—you can still think what you like without consequence."

"Until others learn your thoughts."

"I'll agree with that."

He seemed satisfied with my responses and became silent.

My initial dislike of him decreased but it wasn't entirely gone and I wondered why for he paid one hundred seventy five dollars each session and with his good self-control he was unlikely to cause trouble.

But I couldn't muse more than briefly since there were the necessary questions to be asked at every first session, which he readily answered.

He was sixty four, had never married, and had no children. He completed ROTC at Brown and law school at Harvard before beginning his military career.

He had no previous mental health treatment or significant medical problems. His parents were dead and he had one older sister he rarely saw. He never thought seriously of killing himself or anyone else. He had smoked until he was fifty four, and didn't use drugs or drink more than is considered healthy ("A glass—they say Eisenhower wouldn't have had his heart attack if he had wine that evening").

So he was symptom-free. *Except* for a fear which he wouldn't describe, and because *no one* enters a psychiatrist's office unless they're very distressed. Who else would share their personal secrets with a stranger?

The session moved quickly and he paid me immediately after hearing my closing phrase and even before my usual ending-first-session joke: that the (toy) guns in the corner were to insure payment. Which I said anyway, though the timing was off and this is everything with jokes.

Telling stories and jokes to a captive audience is one of the few ethical perks for a psychiatrist. We scheduled an appointment for the following week and he left after a slight smile, not shaking hands. Apparently, like me, he avoided casual physical contact.

My work day was over, I locked the outside door to my office, and my daily discontent again began. Interesting, excessive work can't completely dim loneliness as I had told to countless patients, though it did succeed for many of my forty seven years.

I was getting lonelier and more rigid though likely no one sensed the latter and my child patients still felt that I was the silliest adult they knew. As I would remain until they wheeled me out.

And I was *dateless*. A quaint word I used only to myself for it identified me as growing up in those years when not having a weekend date was shameful (Saturday night being worse than Friday night), my discomfort disappearing when I became the one who evaluated others.

A girlfriend in medical school told me, "You'll spend your life analyzing it," and I have: studying lives, searching for life, my empty heart filled with the passions of others.

CHAPTER TWO

I WAS IN a room filled with people. Seated as if I were waiting for a movie to start though it was an execution which we were there to witness. Front and center was an electric chair: a horror which I viewed only through the corner of my eye, fearing that if I looked directly at it I would implode. Then I sensed that I was an executioner-in-training and so *must* assist. My panic increased as the warden spoke in a matter-of-fact manner. Without conscious control my head turned and, as I saw the electric chair, I suddenly awoke, soaking with perspiration.

I had left the lights on when I napped but, again, it didn't matter: my nightmare was back. Though I called it *mine,* it had really controlled me, ever since I was five. Even years of psychoanalysis couldn't erase its power.

Every doctor had said that the recurring dream symbolized something important which I must realize and that it would disappear once I did. Which I already knew.

I tried the most logical interpretation: that the electrocution represented my simultaneous need to and fear of viewing my life as it really was, which included my fear of feelings. Still, it persisted.

So I gave up on psychotherapy believing, despite my optimism about others' lives, that maybe, for me, some changes *couldn't be made*. And thereafter I relied on mechanical methods like leaving the lights on and closet doors open before going to sleep.

It wasn't as bad as it once was. Then I would awake in panic, being afraid to return to sleep, finally covering my head with a blanket as do terrified children.

By the time I returned to New York City the nightmare decreased to once or twice a month, I could fall back to sleep in minutes and needed to leave only one light on. But all of the closet doors had to be open, and within a night table lay a loaded British World War Two army issue .455 Webley revolver. A large heavy gun of obsolete caliber and style owned mostly by firearms collectors. This behavior, I knew, was *really* crazy, for how could a gun protect one against a dream?

It was early evening and my dream had occurred for the first time during a daytime nap. It appeared to be strengthening again, with even these hours no longer existing free from my painful fantasy.

I lived in an apartment combined with my office, the city equivalent of suburban physicians who practice in their homes. While they arrange this for convenience, psychiatrists in New York City do so because of the high rents and reduced insurance payments.

But I couldn't complain about money: child psychiatrists were always in demand and I didn't need to impress my young patients with expensive clothes which, unless they were unusually shabby, would pass unnoticed by the adults. My hobbies were also inexpensive; and I hadn't been involved with a woman for too long.

New York is the most expensive place to date. In small towns there is less emphasis on going to the newest restaurant or play. You talked to a woman, then slept with her and melded lives. Staying together from the powerful need for emotional support and the pain of a living a solitary life. I had never married and seemed to couple mostly with divorced women who sensed that if they pressured me for commitment I would flee. My involvement with their children substituted for those I never bore.

But meeting women in New York City wasn't easy. I tried answering personal ads until learning of a colleague who met his ex-patient through one. Thereafter, I only wrote them and all of my attempts were unsuccessful.

Today there's a choice of where to advertise. Years ago there was, largely, *New York* magazine. The *New York Review of Books* and *National Review* also took ads. But these were niche publications and, though regarding myself as "offbeat" (would anyone describe himself as "a typical psychiatrist"?) , mine wasn't the same as theirs.

So I tried *New York*'s Strictly Personals column, writing the ad while munching on my beloved Mallomar cookies. These had been forbidden to me as a child and later became the guilt ridden refuge from my low-fat diet after I graduated from medical school. I labored over each word and wondering how it would sound to the lover I sought.

I considered that some facts were essential for me to include. That I was forty seven, tall, and a psychiatrist. And that I was Jewish but adding "not religious," for no devout woman would be attracted to me and I wouldn't be interested in her. Though with most of the woman I had dated the difference in our religions was easier to cope with than they being liars or hysterical.

I feared to add other details. Would saying that I looked younger than my age make me an "ageist?" Or that I had no interest in sports and loved some movies and TV, a "couch potato?" So I left these details out, jazzed up the heading ("Offbeat Shrink Needs a Fix"), phoned it in paying the two hundred eighty dollar charge with MasterCard, and hoped for the best.

Periodically I ran the same ad and some women responded again though, often, with different facts. I learned that even getting a photo didn't protect you from unwelcome surprises though women had the same experience.

One woman, who was five feet nine inches and liking taller men, told me that a date said he was six feet: when they met *she* was taller than him.

Though these attempts were unsuccessful, I continued them, seeking the happy family life which many achieve but had thus far escaped me. My hopes were high with Amy. She was tall and lithe, well-dressed, soft-spoken, and far more attractive than I had expected. I was glad that I called her even without receiving her photo: I usually discarded letters which didn't contain one. But I was lonely and she was certainly intelligent. She had a Ph. D. in biophysics and worked at a pharmaceutical research company in New Jersey.

Over the phone we compared interests and dislikes, then arranged to meet at a small Greek restaurant on West Forty Eighth Street. I first discovered it soon after returning to the City. A year later, its prices nearly doubled after it was praised in a *Times* review.

We drank wine and ate avgolemono (lemon soup) and spanakopeta (spinach pie). I told my usual first date stories which, because of repetition, no longer felt intimate. I hoped that she was the woman I would stay with. Until I became curious.

"Why is it you never married?"

"I *am* married," she said.

"So *why* are you meeting me?" I asked. Feeling once again that disappointment which would occur when the—alas—too frequent thought again went through my mind: "*another* crazy."

"Things aren't good with my husband. We have a twelve year old and don't want to divorce until he's older. I'm looking for someone to be with now and for me to marry someday."

Even after that wasted evening I didn't give up on personal ads though I did conclude that the most important things about whether a couple will "hit it off" can't be told from a letter or phone call or photo or even from having had all three.

When you meet a stranger you quickly get information which is summarized in the nearly instantaneous conclusion that you *might* be compatible but not whether you *are*. That decision takes more contact.

And it's not their looks. I had the most profound sexual experience (five acts of intercourse in one night!) with a barely attractive woman yet I was once impotent with a true beauty. But even with all my sophisticated knowledge, which included the common belief that it was more romantic to meet spontaneously than through a personal ad, I still couldn't figure out how to do so, though others seemed to know.

Years before, I had a much older friend who found dates by using a camera. He would stroll, notice a stunner walking her dog, and ask if he could photograph it. She usually agreed. Then he would give the woman his business card and say for her to call if she wanted a copy of the photo. They almost always did. Note that he didn't frighten the woman by asking for *her* number.

He also met women by taking ballet dance notation lessons. Being the only affluent male there he was much in demand.

I even tried the bar scene for the first time, wandering into one for several inane conversations, and then going to another nearby. After speaking with a guy about the difficult housing situation—for there were no women present— I asked when they usually arrived. His reaction made me realize that I was in a gay bar.

So while I wasn't optimistic about bars, Khristina's was different for it was across town. On Sixty Ninth Street and Madison Avenue, one of the most affluent areas of the city and, psychologically, a world away from where I lived.

It was divided into a Swedish (mostly fish) restaurant, and a bar with tables, club chairs, and a studio piano which was played between nine and eleven in the evening. Having only chairs and small tables, this was an area for talking not eating, though I once cadged coffee from the bartender. That it was never crowded was unusual for expatriates often developed drinking problems when they were away from Sweden's high liquor taxes.

The city's noise barely penetrated the darkened lounge, making it easy to let sips of Hennessy Cognac and the languorous piano music take effect. Though, later, I still had to return home bearing my unchanged life, regardless of whether I was ready to face the next working day.

Once the world did intrude. An apron caught fire and I was forced to practice the emergency medicine which I had mostly forgotten since my internship. After which I was offered a free drink (as were all of the customers) and appointed the Restaurant's Chief Physician. Which entitled me to—the reward was unspecified.

It was during that dinner when I first noticed Gerri —and her two daughters who were being impossible. Both were blond too, one about three, the other four. The older wore blue jeans and a T-shirt emblazoned with Bugs Bunny, the younger, a dress with flowers and ruffles. Their behavior was equally different: the younger ate daintily, the older with her fingers like an infant.

Gerri wore black jeans and T-shirt. Her ski-jacket and those of the children and their backpacks lay on empty chairs: Khristina's was unusually responsive to the needs of parents for a New York restaurant.

My table was close beside theirs. I noted the lack of a wedding ring on Gerri's finger (though I also knew this indicator of availability could be misleading). I quickly "made my move" as my friend of the dog picture taking/dance notation class pickup experiences had always advised.

"Three and four?" I asked, wanting to indicate that I related well to children. Her faint smile contained accepting exasperation.

"Three and five. Kirsten is three and acts like she is going on thirteen. Five year old Karen is her sister."

Kirsten preened as her sister ignored me. My elderly friend had said to never let the conversation flag, and to keep dropping details which emphasized respectability.

"I'm a psychiatrist and work with kids but I'm not good at guessing their age. Once, at a party in a wealthy couple's apartment, I fantasized about all of the rich patients I'd get, tried showing how much I knew and asked, 'Is your son five?' 'She's six,' the father said. But that girl had short-cut hair and was dressed like a boy. I'm still leery about guessing children's' ages but am sure that both of yours are girls."

As we spoke her children listened, no longer playing with their food.

"Geraldine Karlstrennes. With one 'K,' two 'e's' and two 'n's," she said, smiling and extending her hand.

"Lew Yungg," I responded, "with a 'u' not 'o-u' and two 'g's,' though I've thought of changing it. People expect me to be the wise but inscrutable Charlie Chan. Yungg is a corruption of some German name. The immigration officers were being playful. Why were you named Geraldine —though it's pretty and connotes stability."

"I try to be though with the kids I don't often achieve it. The short story is that my mother is English. The longer is too long with them being here."

By then her children had lost interest in us and turned back to their food.

"Maybe now we have time," I said.

"My father wanted a son as the first child. He was to man the archetypal fishing boat which the family had lost four generations back and the last time that a boy was born. When my mother became pregnant, relatives advised folk remedies she agreed to try but ignored. Though assuring them that the baby would be named *Gerald* to honor a dead relative. So only *Geraldine* became possible.

"Where did you learn to speak English. You talk it better than me."

"School, and my mother spoke it to us. I grew up just a little more Danish. I've read that you dream in the language you're most comfortable with and sometimes I dream in English."

"I guess."

My nightmare had occurred that day so dreams weren't my favorite topic of conversation.

Neither of us noticed the rumpus until we saw diners watching. Karen was kicking her sister and Kirsten seemed about to escalate the conflict by throwing food— until the children saw Gerri stare. The fighting stopped. They didn't like sharing their mother's attention and had gotten it back.

"It looks like their mealtime is over."

"I've enjoyed speaking with you," I said quickly. "How about dinner this weekend?"

She paused and I again lost hope, as I had so often in my life.

"It's probably all right but I can't be sure about a baby-sitter now." Which statement produced a scream from Karen that she wasn't a baby. "Call me," Gerri said, taking a card from a black leather case. I gave her mine after scribbling my home phone number on it.

"You *are* a psychiatrist—you don't look like one."

"That's what my dentist says but he's not a typical dentist so I don't always believe him. I stopped wearing black suits when I left Chicago. I'll tell you about it tomorrow."

"I try not to be typical either," she said with a smile.

As she stood, I realized that she was only three inches shorter than my six feet two inches, and almost too thin.

The rest of my meal was dull.

Back to loneliness.

CHAPTER THREE

I<small>T WAS A</small> typical working Saturday, with all of my patients being children.

A girl whose failing grades were driving her parents crazy. An angry eighteen year old, jailed on a minor charge, who told his embarrassed police chief/father that he would "sooner stay in jail" than be transferred to the psychiatric hospital which strings were being pulled to arrange.

A ballsy five year old with nightmares who was in a, so to speak, knock-down/drag-out fight with her stepfather. A year before she had wanted to kiss a boy who didn't want to be kissed. So she started a girl gang, gave stick-on tattoos to signify membership, and then ordered them to hold him down while she kissed him.

Finally, an eight year old with stomach problems who played video games in his room and cried when being forced by his parents to socialize.

By one o'clock my working week was over. I locked the door to the waiting room and took a nap. Having once again found myself practicing chic behavior by doing what I long did: eating healthy, and taking naps.

Since I was always a poor sleeper, I found that if I didn't nap I would increasingly resent patients as the day wore on—which is a quick way to ruin a business and no way to run it. Only after my Saturday siesta did I feel that my working week was really over, though now I had a new nightmare.

I was walking along dark and lonely streets, seeking a book. Then I sensed that I was being followed and used a blackjack to smash the window of a parked car, which I hot-wired and drove to a library. But the volume I opened was written in German which I barely understood.

I left the library feeling confident, even as large men holding chains surrounded me. They began beating me and I woke in panic, fearing that I had overslept and missed scheduled patients. Then I realized it was Saturday afternoon and calmed down.

I couldn't figure out the dream. Loneliness was a hallmark of my life but why was I carrying a blackjack and the book written in German? I always told children that scary dreams are like mystery movies which should be interpreted but not feared. So I tried to do this but was unsuccessful, and consoled myself with the thought that some dreams are best solved by letting one's unconscious mind work on them.

Tonight was my date with Geraldine, or Gerri as she preferred to be called, and I phoned to confirm it.

"I'm calling to check that you got a baby-sitter."

"I did, though I'm not sure who's doing the hiring. Manhattan teens have money so you have to be on *their* list. She's fifteen and sometimes only a little more grown up than the kids. But she lives in the next building so I don't have to pay for her taxi fare home too. Now it's eight dollars an hour per child. *With complaints* if more is asked than plopping on the sofa to watch TV—hopefully with their boyfriend."

"I'll pay. I didn't realize how much it costs."

"They're my responsibility but you can buy dinner."

"What kind of food do you like?"

"Any is fine. We ate out yesterday but usually don't. It's too much hassle with them. Do you have kids?"

"None, though a friend first learned about his son when the boy was in high school. I can't imagine why the mother waited so long to tell him."

"Maybe she was afraid that he'd seek custody."

"It could be."

I wanted to continue chatting but was leery of too long first-time phone conversations: these could easily lead to a premature sharing of secrets and for the relationship to end quickly. So I returned to the mechanics of our date. Or did I *really* fear our increasing rapport as we spoke?

"Have you ever had Uzbekistan food?"

"Where's that?"

"A former Russian province. The restaurant got a 'GO' signal in *FORBES* so it can't be too offbeat."

"Sounds good."

"Seven OK?"

"You bet. I'm at Twelve-O-Four East Fifty First, Twenty Nine D—turn right when you leave the elevator."

Soon after I hung up the phone, feeling relaxed and drinking a Diet Cherry Coke, I realized a little of what today's dream was trying to tell me. That sometimes what I believed to be true was very wrong indeed.

CHAPTER FOUR

GERRI LIVED IN Beekman Place, a six block area along the East River just north of the United Nations complex. It was a quiet neighborhood with several brownstones being used as consulates or ambassadorial residences. The largest apartment houses had art-deco features and were built in the nineteen thirties; her's was an undistinguished boxy building constructed thirty years later.

I arrived ten minutes early and stood outside the building . Then, with more anxiety than I felt I should before a date at my age, I gave the doorman my name and rode the elevator to the twenty ninth floor. Where Gerri stood beside her open door, dressed in jeans and a pink blouse. Her slim body and sharply etched features caused her casual clothes to seem elegant. The children's screams disturbed my fantasy of undressing her.

"They've been like this since they heard I was going out."

"Maybe it's how I look," I said. Adding, since she wasn't yet accustomed to my offbeat humor, "just joking."

"I knew you were. I don't know what it is—possibly having just me and being afraid to lose me. But they liked you so maybe it'll be easier tonight."

The apartment's foyer led to a living-room where her upset children were enmeshed with stuffed animals, puzzles, and coloring books.

"Lew's here. Remember—you met him at the restaurant," she said.

They cried louder. I felt rejected even though I knew better.

"How about wine?" Gerri offered.

"OK."

"Red or white?"

"It doesn't matter."

She nodded as if to say, "I know it can be hard dealing with the children of a date."

After she left, I sat down on the sofa and picked up a stuffed bear which lay on its side.

"What's his name?"

"It's girl," three year old Kirsten replied.

"What's *her* name?" I persisted.

"Beauty."

"*Wow.* That's a really nice name for a bear," I said loudly, with as much emotion as I could muster. An adult must behave dramatically to get a child's attention. Then I quickly added, so as not to lose it, "How old is she?"

"Don't know." While she spoke, her older sister watched silently.

"She looks like a baby but will probably be really big when she grows up. Do you want to do a puzzle or color?"

"Puzzle," said Kirsten. "I want to color," insisted the older Karen, "so we'll color." Hearing this, her sister began crying again.

"Let's do a puzzle *and* color," I suggested, trying to defuse the situation by getting us active. I had Kirsten choose a puzzle and Karen a coloring book. Soon they were busy and I complimented both on their skills. Upon her return, Gerri didn't comment on their improved behavior. That would have set them off again.

"Red it is," she said. "With goat cheese. We like it but it may be an acquired taste."

"I *don't* like it," Karen said.

"I'll try it and see if it's yucky. If it is, then..." and produced my sound of an upset elephant. Both smiled and resumed their activities. I knew the cheese wasn't yucky, having loved it before I became obsessed with following a low-fat diet.

We drank and watched the children. Then Gerri showed me the apartment.

"This room is theirs. I try to get them to keep their things in it. I've become what I vowed never to be: a mother obsessed with neatness."

"Like most mothers. There's nothing wrong with that but it's important to recognize a kid's limits. They'll usually do what you ask unless they're tired or angry. Or they have some reason not to, one which makes sense only to them. Then it's best to let things go. Sorry—I'm being a psychiatrist."

"Maybe I'm pushing for free advice. Let me show you where I work when I can get free of them."

Her room was about fourteen by sixteen. Along one wall was a black leather sofa, likely a sofa bed. Opposite was a computer, laser printer, and fax machine, with their jumble of cables. Bookshelves lined other walls and journals overflowed tan rattan baskets on the floor.

"What do you do?" I asked, reading the titles.

"Market research with kids. Companies hire me to find out what they want to buy."

"Why? How much money could they have?"

"More than you realize. To spend on whatever they want without having to worry about rent or food. Over a hundred billion a year if you include what they hassle their parents for. A company which gets just a tiny piece of this market does OK."

I wanted to know more but one of the children started crying.

"I'll call to see what's keeping the sitter," she said.

We went to her kitchen, which was typical of those in City apartments. Despite its tiny size it had a feature which New Yorkers prize though is commonplace for other Americans: a window. Many City kitchens have only air vents.

"I'll go back to my puzzle and coloring."

"I'm sorry. I expected that we'd be gone by now."

"It's OK. I enjoy being silly with normal kids and not having to worry whether it's in their best therapeutic interest."

The crying stopped when I entered the living room. Now both children self-consciously ignored me, Kirsten working at her puzzle and Karen coloring.

I sipped wine, feeling more comfortable than in years. Having closeness is important, I told myself, not keeping secrets. I was so tired of having to keep secrets.

Karen's soft voice interrupted my thinking. "Daddy died and it broke me and mommy's heart."

"I'm sorry. I didn't know. That's very sad," I said, no longer being just a relaxed observer. She resumed coloring as Gerri approached the sofa.

"A problem with her makeup. She'll be here soon."

Karen looked distressed, "I told him about daddy."

"I appreciated learning that he died," I said quickly. "It must be hard for everyone."

Gerri toyed with her wine, drank a little and put it down, then cradled the glass in her hands before drinking more.

"We've been doing OK for seven months, haven't we girls?" she insisted.

They ignored her. Like most psychiatrists I pride myself on knowing when not to speak and followed one of my professional mottoes: "When you're unsure what to say, don't say it."

The doorbell rang and Gerri soon returned with the baby-sitter, who looked more twenty than fifteen. Her black hair reached the small of her back. She wore deep red lipstick and blue mascara, red jeans and multicolored platform shoes. Her white top revealed her midriff and barely contained her well developed breasts. She was bubbly and I felt old and wondered what had happened to my life.

Plopping on the floor and gushing over the girls, she asked if they wanted ice cream sodas. During their ensuing love fest, Gerri said that she would be back by midnight and to page her if a problem developed. They barely noticed our leaving.

In the elevator, Gerri asked, "Where's the restaurant?"

"On Sixty Third and First. I thought that we'd walk there unless you're tired."

"I'm not, and I like walking."

She slipped her arm through mine and we went several blocks in a comfortable silence.

"I was sorry to hear about the death of your husband."

"You needn't be," she responded angrily. "If the bastard wasn't dead I would have killed him."

CHAPTER FIVE

THE SLUM BUILDINGS on Sixty Third Street and First Avenue are inhabited by generations of families who became frozen in place by rent-control regulations. A phenomenon most common in New York City where one family may pay ten times their neighbor's rent. So, seated on stoops or looking out their windows on this warm night, were people whose dress resembled more their impoverished ancestors than that embraced by the recipients of Wall Street's prosperity.

The restaurant, Itchan Kala, was named (according to the menu) after an ancient cultural site in Uzbekistan. It had five tables in its center and twelve booths along two walls. The floors were hardwood with black lace curtains covering the windows. Medieval type tapestries which portrayed hunting scenes hung from the walls. Songs from an old Rodgers and Hart musical, *The Boys From Syracuse*, alternated with those from The Carpenters and Gilbert O'Sullivan.

The waiters were Sikh, with their ethnicity being easily identified by beards and turbans.

With all this discordance I wondered about the good *Forbes* review but need not have. The restaurant was as competently managed as are most Indian ones, and despite their youth the waiters were continuously attentive.

We didn't speak further after her angry outburst. This wasn't completely comfortable but I knew that developing a relationship took time and I already liked her and the children. Even their apartment with its typical Scandinavian furnishings, lacking only the usual door curtain to keep out drafts. I wanted to know more but didn't know how ask or to end the increasingly heavy silence between us. So I waited until she did.

"What do you want to know? You have twenty questions about me."

"Only twenty?"

She didn't say anything and I sensed that my jocular words were intended, unconsciously, to push her away.

"I'm sorry. I avoid asking questions in social situations. People think that they're being diagnosed."

"Then start with five."

"How long were you married?"

"For seven years. We lived together four years before. His name was Siggie, short for Sigmund. We got married when I wanted kids—which he didn't and never got much involved with."

"What kind of work did he do?"

"He was a futurist which is basically a researcher and thinker. He was originally a computer programmer with a Ph. D. in experimental psychology. He worked for a conglomerate owned by Kirsten's godfather before going out to consult on his own. He was very capable when he wasn't drinking."

"He died young."

"At thirty seven. I'm forty one."

"I didn't ask your age."

"But you wondered, like all Americans do. Only here is a person's age so often listed next to their name. Check the *Wall Street Journal* sometime."

"What caused his death?"

"The usual stupid drunk driving. His car went off the road during a business trip in Florida. It's not a nice ending."

"No."

"Maybe I'll never tell the kids."

"Just a car accident."

"The woman with him was my best friend and they shared a room. That was another shock."

"Yes."

She looked down at the table for several moments, then up at me. "It was like Siggie not to have insurance. Either he thought that he'd live forever or didn't care enough. I've tried building my business but ad agencies think only young people can be creative. Not someone over forty."

She toyed with a packet of crackers before continuing. "Some months we just scrape by though the kids don't know. Kirsten's godfather sends them gifts every other month. He'd send weekly if I let him."

"Why don't you?"

"I don't want them getting used to expensive things rather than what I can provide. I do let him pay for day care and medical bills. He'd insist and rich people usually get their way. But he means well. His parents and sister were killed in the Holocaust and kids are important to him. He's Jewish."

"How did he get so wealthy?"

"It wasn't hard during the Cold War if you were bright and without scruples. But he's good underneath."

Our orders arrived. Despite its ethnicity the restaurant, in breadth of dishes, resembled more a typical New York diner, which were once owned mostly by Greeks and now by Indians. The menu listed the ingredients beside each dish, which seemed a good idea.

I had Egyptian Kebabs (chicken breasts, yogurt, turmeric, curry powder, onions, tomatoes, lemon juice, cardamom, salt); Gerri had Chicken A La Kiev (chicken, butter, chives, flour, eggs, bread crumbs, black pepper, salt, fried in soybean oil).

We left the restaurant at eleven and spoke little as we walked back to her apartment.

"Want to come up for coffee?"

"OK."

"The girls should be sleeping though I make no promise."

They were dozing on the sofa while the baby-sitter talked on the phone to "CJ." She waved as we came in, and quickly dropping the receiver.

"It wasn't long distance."

"I know. I trust you," Gerri said.

She paid the baby-sitter who smiled knowingly at us before leaving. I wouldn't have trusted myself to see her home. After the children were placed in their beds we sat drinking coffee.

"Can you stay?"

"I'd like to but I get scared when kids are around. Once a three old got up in the middle of the night, barged into her mother's room, saw us naked and asked, 'What's *he* doing here?' She said, 'He was tired and went to bed.' The girl stared, 'If he was tired why didn't he go home?' It traumatized me."

"You shock easily."

"I like to tell stories. Sometimes I add lines so they play better."

She put down her cup and leaned back on the sofa. I put my arm about her, drew her closer and kissed her. Her lips parted and I explored her mouth with my tongue. It tasted of coffee. She moved her head and whispered, "Put down your cup." I did. Then I kissed her again and gently fingered her nipples, feeling them harden.

She pushed her body against mine and I rubbed her crotch, first softly then persistently. As she was opening my belt a shriek burst from the bedroom.

"Kirsten wet the bed again!"

"I'll be there in a minute!"

38

"I better get going."

"You don't have to and you don't have to be nervous —not all girls wet the bed."

I was, though she didn't.

I left at four before the children were up. It was too early in our relationship for me to "play daddy." We held each other and I promised to call that evening. Despite the early hour, getting a taxi to the West Side was no problem. As it hurtled through the empty streets, I lay sprawled in the cushions, feeling more relaxed than I had in years as I remembered what an elderly psychiatrist had once told me: that having sex is the best sleeping pill.

CHAPTER SIX

To my surprise, I did call Gerri that night. Many failed relationships had taught me that women prize reliability above all, and I hoped to change my ways.

"What time did you get up?" I asked.

"Six thirty with the kids. I napped during their play date."

"I nap too. I couldn't survive my schedule without it."

"Can you reduce it?"

"If you don't accept new patients, you stop getting referrals."

"That makes sense."

"Yeah, but without a family you tend to work too much. How's your dating schedule."

"Completely open."

"I'm already more relaxed. How about seeing a movie tomorrow?"

"We don't have to go out. You haven't experienced my cooking. Come at eight when the kids will be out of their bath and calmer."

That's how it started. My being back into what I considered a Midwest—not New York City—relationship, but was really just the normal family life I had repeatedly gained and then lost.

A very smart friend told me that when you are involved in craziness it seems so true but later you wonder how you could have believed what you once did. Now, having Gerri and the kids, I realized that this observation also related to me. I was content until I met them but then wondered how I tolerated my previous solitary life.

But having kids *was* tiring. My sleeping time became reduced as I got up earlier to have more time alone with Gerri before her daughters' demands consumed us. They were fun times, but still intrusive ones.

Differences between us soon arose. Europeans are surprised at how freely Americans talk about sex despite being so guarded about income. So maybe it was only natural that our first friction began over money, and this was after we had sex.

"I had a dream last night," she said.

"I know. You were thrashing and mumbling. I held you and you fell back to sleep."

"I was talking to Siggie who couldn't hear me. Then a boulder rolled towards me."

"It sounds like you were trying to reach him and couldn't."

"We never could talk. But why the boulder?"

"Possibly you feel that arguing is dangerous, though you do with me."

"Maybe just with you. Now we have to talk—I have a problem."

"You've come to the right person."

"Be serious."

"What's up doc?"

"Now the cartoon bunny."

"I'll stop. What's bothering you?"

"Paying rent. My business is barely covering our expenses."

I *wanted* to say, "Don't worry—we'll share," as I felt closer even than when I was inside of her earlier. But she noticed my hesitation.

"What's wrong?" she asked, stroking my cheek as I faced away from her, just as do psychoanalytic patients with their doctor.

"I'm scared."

"Of *me*?"

I was afraid to speak for too often my unthinking words had killed past relationships. But I also knew that if I remained silent our relationship would begin to unravel.

The problem was that I never trusted anyone and, in past relationships, had merely played at being husband and father. Now part of me—but only part—*did want commitment.*

"You don't frighten me," I lied. But she sensed this, and drew away.

"My problems aren't yours."

"I *want* to help and am mostly living here. I'll open a checking account for you and deposit four thousand dollars each month. Ask if you need more."

It was all that I could say. She seemed to sense this and again stroked my cheek. I rubbed her back and between her legs, trying to ignore the gulf between us by reaching her sexually. Which didn't work as it rarely does. Like I tell couples: when something is wrong in a relationship, sex is the first thing to go. Thankfully, we quickly fell asleep.

I felt thankful in the morning: our relationship had survived its first crisis. Maybe this problem wouldn't have been a big one for most couples. But sharing implied commitment, which was difficult for this middle-aged, heterosexual, never married, reasonably attractive, financially solvent guy.

The stockbroker wife of my cardiologist friend joked that such a guy was so rare in New York she could make a fortune incorporating me and selling stock. Maybe. Until buyers read the prospectus.

But I also had to earn a living though now this was only part of my life, and one which I tried to forget at night.

CHAPTER SEVEN

MY FIRST PATIENT on Monday was the Reverend Cary McMasterby: parish priest, noted speaker, and seducer of young pretty women. He kept our appointments religiously (to use a bad pun) during his first months of treatment and, so far as I knew, kept his hands off all women too, including his wife. He related his extramarital behavior to her understandable aversion: not many petite women with six foot four inch husbands welcomed anal sex.

"How were things this week?" I asked. This was the more common of my two introductions, the other being silence until the patient spoke.

"Better. Yesterday's sermon achieved a rousing reception—*everyone* stayed awake!"

Cary's development of a sense of humor indicated his increased ability to consider his behavior, which indicated his improvement.

"What was it about?" I asked, thinking if his greatest hope was that I agreed with his grandiose image of himself, his second was to baptize me into his faith.

"A usually boring topic: theology. People like being told wealth is achievable and God loves them but not that."

"What *is* theology?"

"That's a good question. It's the science of God: the clearest and most accurate ideas we have about Him. I gave this sermon for the first time in Vietnam after a sergeant told me he had no use for theology. He knew who God was when he was alone at night and experiencing His mystery."

"What did you reply?"

"Nothing. I just wondered what we were both doing in that godforsaken place."

"Do you agree with him now?"

"No. I think those people are turning away from the real to something less substantial. Compare the actual Pacific to a map. The ocean has a powerful, immediate effect but the map is based on the views of thousands of observers. Which is more authentic?

Theology provides the answers to eternal questions from within a religious framework. Ignoring dogma forces each person to begin anew. Like a statistician who would have to invent a new formula for each problem if he were to ignore those of past experts."

"And a psychologist who uses tests to compare a patient's responses with those from very many others, not only those he treated."

Cary smiled. "Which is just the conclusion that I would like my parishioners to grasp."

I thought for a moment, and then tried to learn more about his background.

"How long are you at your present parish?"

"Eleven years."

"How many posts did you have before that one?"

"Two. The first was a one year tryout which didn't work. It was called a church but really was a religiously oriented 'Y' where I was expected to be the minister/cheerleader/administrator who regularly called upon God to benefit members as citizens, workers, or family participants.

"Their last minister was a scholar. After he died they wanted someone different, hired me, and are still looking. At some congregations a little scholarship goes a long way. My next one lasted eight years."

"How was it there?"

"The New Testament says that everyone should work to be able to help the needy. I was certainly poor, and they wanted a war hero or someone they thought was one—they take the military seriously in Texas.

"I wasn't a bad choice but what they really wanted was a fundamentalist and I'm...what would you call me?"

"A complicated guy."

"A freethinker who has a hard time meshing with parishioners. Now I complain because most aren't interested in dogma. There, I didn't teach what they wanted. So after two, three year contract extensions I was offered only one year and took the hint. Along with a tin parachute: nine months salary and medical benefits to leave quietly. A wealthy member recently asked if I'd be interested in returning. There are styles in pastoring like with psychotherapy. Maybe we're both coming back."

"Long ago a psychologist told me that people have to get back to psychoanalytic thinking because nowhere else can they understand their lives."

46

"People need more than a 'Y,'" Cary nodded. "There'll always be some who want only child care and support towards conventional success but that's not my type of religion.

"I seem to be an old-fashioned preacher from the eighteen hundreds. The most popular recent religions had roots in communism or fascism. Which were *abominations* —but potent because of the good they imitated to societies starved for it. Like giving people a sense of belonging and enough food."

"Does psychotherapy conflict with your beliefs?"

Cary smiled.

"Might it might interfere with your work?" I pressed.

Now he smiled more broadly, as if knowing that I would eventually ask this.

"You're taking me seriously," he said.

"I always take you seriously."

"As a patient—not like my work had the value of yours. But now your condescension is gone and you're wondering. Which is the first step to faith."

I looked at the darkening sky. Hopefully it would rain and cool the weather. I was having an ongoing war with Gerri over the air conditioning setting, I liking it cooler and the kids refusing to take sides.

This was yet another friction between us. I smiled at my "hope" that it would rain—maybe treating Cary *was* beginning to effect me.

I returned from my reverie.

"Do you believe that psychotherapy and religion conflict?" I repeated.

Now he sprawled in his chair, and looked more relaxed than in past sessions.

"They're concerned with different things," he replied. "When a person makes a moral choice—you may object to the word *moral*—two issues are involved. Choosing, and the emotions causing it. Which I'll admit derive from childhood and can be unconscious. Psychoanalysis is concerned with motives and feelings, Christianity with choice.

"For a true Christian even anxiety contains an element of faith: that one is sharing the passion of Christ who knew where his behavior led and prayed the inevitable wouldn't happen while knowing that it must."

"A psychiatrist would say that the presence of anxiety indicates conflict."

"A minister, that anxiety must be understood in terms of inner turmoil. Which can have a psychological *or* religious basis."

We were talked out. Every psychotherapy session is a battle between the patient's unconscious and their doctor's push towards developing greater self-control and understanding. Since treatment began we had boxed back and forth, Cary's anger at my power over his career being visible in his frequent brief, sarcastic responses. Which were matched by my not always successful hiding of contempt for his past inappropriate behavior.

But I also feared his rage for he was two inches taller and thirty pounds heavier than me. Those times, when I found myself thinking of the Webley revolver several rooms away, I told myself that I was anxious because I sensed his anger was increasing. Which, I knew, *must* happen during psychotherapy since only through this process could one develop greater self-control. Yet only slowly did I begin liking him and respecting his struggle, as I did those of my other patients.

I reminded myself that my goal was to heal, and remembered Cary's words that a person cannot understand the true meaning of God until he is conscious of sin and the incredibly mean and ugly behavior which humans can do.

CHAPTER EIGHT

LAURA OWNED A business specializing in notions which are objects ranging from buttons to sequins and anything else which is capable of beautifying clothing.

Though men gaped at her short skirts and intense make-up, her sex life was so minimal that I offered my usual joke for this circumstance: questioning whether she saved intimacy for July 4th as a patriotic gesture.

But it was the panic attacks which brought her to therapy. First, being afraid that she would faint in the supermarket; later, at her office; finally, even at home.

I treated her symptoms with a deliberate matter-of-fact attitude by giving information about anxiety and how it was impossible to die from. Soon she described the physical abuse by her father, and her teenage flight to Houston where she worked as an "exotic dancer."

Laura eventually returned to school while living with a widowed college teacher who became the nurturing parent she needed. After graduation, and recognizing her just average clothing design ability, she moved to New York City and began her successful business. She married a TV producer and had three daughters.

Fifteen years later they divorced when he decided that he was gay. She met her present husband, Carl, a policeman, when he threatened to give her a parking ticket.

Laura's current problem were the pornographic magazines which Carl left in the downstairs bathroom which was sometimes used by her daughters.

Ordinarily I would have met with both of them several times, advised the need for personal privacy, and then never spoken with him again particularly since I ranked in Carl's estimation with his bookie, who had disappeared to avoid paying a five figure win.

Carl felt that we both stole his money, ignoring the fact that Laura's income (which paid for her therapy) was four times his. I joked that he should have let the Mob which produced his pornography also handle his betting since they always paid off. Or they did in those days when it was still well organized.

The day went quickly and soon Harold ("The General") arrived. He shared information which I would have expected to learn only from books describing the work of the many investigating committees he served on, for he had long been valued by both political parties for his ability to sense when something was incomplete or untrue.

But the stories he told, of senators and presidents, had the same intent as those of the insurance salesmen I treated (who are *great* story tellers): his unconscious desire to be an interesting and thus presumably valued patient until he felt comfortable enough to share his *real* concerns with me.

"When you speak with a president," he said, "you must separate the man from the myth. Which can be difficult since by addressing him as 'Mr. President' you invest him with greatness. You try not to let yourself be talked into something but it's not easy when 'the president' asks. Johnson would throw his arm around you and could talk you into anything. Clinton got close and charmed you —when he wasn't raging.

"But you can't let yourself be intimidated. The greatest benefit I got from a Harvard law degree was that more people were impressed with me than they should have been."

"You've done a lot," I said.

"I kept my mouth shut and so was forgiven when I made mistakes. And I didn't tell reporters about those of others which Americans don't want to know anyway. They need their myth of a paternal government though terrible events can follow the best intentions."

I enjoyed speaking with him and Cary for they were my most articulate patients. But they were *not* paying for friendship and if they sensed that they were getting only this they would quickly end their therapy, as least with me.

I remembered my initial impression of Harold. It was unusual for a sixty four year old who never had mental health treatment to seek it without some external pressure ("my lawyer said it would look better"; "my wife said either I get therapy or she leaves").

If he had tolerated his life for so long, what suddenly made it unbearable? His only symptom was a recurring fear which he still refused to describe.

52

"It's rare for someone beyond their forties to begin psychotherapy," I said. "By then they've adjusted. You've had your nightmare for years so it's not that.

"Some people begin therapy and aren't sure why so they soon drop out. But you're still here, and to achieve your goals we must know them."

Then I mentally kicked myself: "He's paying a hundred seventy five dollars each session and not causing trouble. Why not keep your mouth shut? Is something about him making *you* uncomfortable? And are you dealing with *your* anxiety by causing him to end his treatment? Besides, what's the rush? Your therapy took nine years and you're far from healed."

Finally he spoke, with an undertone of anger, "I don't say anything until I'm sure." Then, calmer, "I don't know who I am."

I felt relieved—maybe my questioning him had been helpful.

"I just want to be sure that I understand you correctly," I said, in a conciliatory tone. "Knowing oneself isn't a black or white affair. Some areas you do, maybe others not. But it's not that you don't know who you are *at all*."

I emphasized this point so Harold didn't feel that he was what is popularly called "crazy." People believing their problems are *really* bad often end treatment abruptly and feel worse than before it began.

"You're right," he said. "I'm used to doing what lawyers do best: manipulate people. Facing up to myself isn't easy."

"It's not for most people until they're forced to do so by a crisis. Or after years of therapy when it's become second nature."

"I suggested that others seek treatment but didn't need a voyeur nosing into *my* life."

"I've been called worse."

"Then Foster killed himself. Though he had a wife and kids."

"Foster?"

"Vincent Foster. Clinton's chief lawyer. He did it in a Washington park, with an old revolver they say."

"Did you know him?"

"Just barely. I heard that he took too seriously what people wrote, not understanding Washington's silliness. Then he ignored every lawyers' basic proverbs: that all clients lie, and their major loyalty must be to themselves."

"Have you always followed these?"

"I try. Once I didn't and it cost me favors. But like lawyers tell people who plead poverty: 'That money you saved for a rainy day—it's raining now!'"

Harold was starting to tell impersonal stories again. However, I had asked a "depth" question, gotten his honest response, and he was still comfortable with therapy. All in all, it was a good session. But why was he so upset by Foster's death when they weren't close?

People kill themselves every day. Did this event arouse Harold's fear of suicide—both were lawyers, and Harold distrusted psychiatrists. Maybe Foster distrusted them too, or *was* he in treatment, this being kept secret after his death?

54

If (as I knew) the CIA had its list of security cleared psychiatrists then surely the White House also did, these being made up of those—nowadays unfortunately—too few doctors who still refused to give interviews.

Probably both had difficulty dealing with their feelings—just like every lawyer I knew. But Harold's motive *couldn't* have been his fear of suicide since he denied this at our first session. Yet Foster's death *must* have motivated his rush into treatment. Why else would he speak of it?

I knew that if Harold continued in therapy these questions would eventually be answered. In any case, his forty five minutes of my time was now up and Harold did say that loyalty to oneself should be first.

CHAPTER NINE

I HAD ALWAYS SOUGHT a life like the fifties TV show *Ozzie And Harriet*. We all need our fantasies to sustain us and mine was that, somewhere, a loving family life awaited me.

But this evening *Lew And Family* wasn't *Ozzie And Harriet*. Karen wouldn't go to bed without her favorite pajamas so Kirsten wouldn't either and she gripped the rug with all of her strength. Gerri had washed the clothes in the sink and was now drying them with a hair dryer, the laundry room being closed for renovation.

She looked frazzled—but beautiful. I immediately wanted to undress her and thought how much easier our life would be without the kids. But I knew that she was a package deal, and remembered what one mother had told her teenager who wanted to live at home while attending college: "I'm paying $21,000/year for you to stay home?!"

Feeling that I needed to do something, I asked Kirsten, "What's wrong?" She only screamed louder. Then, telling myself I was much older and maybe even as smart as she was, I returned to my daytime role of psychiatrist.

"Sometimes children get unhappy and aren't sure why they are. Maybe Karen can't wear her best pajamas. That's *her* problem and mommy will help her. She'll probably get her new ones tomorrow. Do *you* need new pajamas? Do you want to go shopping *too*?"

Kirsten slowly stopped crying and then whispered, "yes," softly into the rug.

"Where's the ice cream? I'm hungry and if my tummy doesn't eat it's gonna start growling. So loud that the police will come and arrest it for making too much noise."

"Silly," she said.

"Sometimes I'm real silly. But I am hungry. Do you know where the ice cream is?"

Soon we were eating, and Karen's crisis was also over.

A few minutes later the kids were asleep. Both were worn out.

"I promised Kirsten new pajamas."

"Anything," she said, brushing strands of hair from her forehead.

"How did your day go?"

"OK, but I can't wait till they start school. Now I can only work when they're in day-care. A check came so I won't need money this month."

"No—I said that I'd give you four thousand dollars each month and that's it. Our life is together."

We sat on the couch. I rubbed her back and kissed her hair. "What was the check for?"

"Doing research on how parents feel about their kids being on the Internet. How did your day go?"

"Thankfully, just the usual. A sudden change means trouble. It's better to be bored. I've handled every kind of crisis but still stay wired until things settle down."

"Sounds like its time for a career change."

"I can't think of anything better. I always complain—too many patients or not enough."

"You aren't so bad," she said, as I licked her neck. "But *don't* give me another hickey. You may feel sixteen but my accounts take me more seriously when they're not smiling at the sight of my neck."

I stopped, got to my knees and lifted her skirt.

"And *you* don't have to *peek*," she said, kissing me.

Next morning the kids were as delightful as they had been difficult the past evening. Karen dressed herself and helped Kirsten. She even got breakfast for both of them. We awoke to the heaven of a quiet apartment.

After they left for preschool, we ate.

"Did you ever hear of Vincent Foster?" I asked.

"The lawyer who killed himself?"

"Yes. What do you know about it?"

"Why do you ask?"

"It came up in conversation." I didn't want to reveal that it was with a patient.

"Not much," she said. "He was Clinton's chief lawyer and lifelong friend. He shot himself and left a torn-up note. They said he was depressed and didn't get treatment. Either he didn't believe in it or was afraid of how it would look. There were lots of rumors."

"About what? Suicide happens everyday."

"That there was a big cover-up: he was murdered and the note was only part of what he wrote. Things are different in Denmark."

"I bet."

"No, really. There the queen walks down the street like a commoner, and people would learn right away if the prime minister lied. Then he'd be out of office the next morning. It's not like Sweden at all."

"What happens there?"

"Like in Washington. The prime minister was murdered with rumors of bribes and arms deals with India. But Foster's death was in all of the papers. How could you miss it?"

"I don't read them or watch the news."

"Why? Don't you feel out of it? How can doctors advertise if they don't know what's bothering people?"

"Fun-nee."

"No," she insisted. "I could understand if you were eighty and withdrawing from life. But sometimes you act sixteen—or four."

How much should I tell her? And if she knew, would she stay or, someday, use the knowledge against me? But it could have happened to anyone. "It was just your bad luck," the detective had said, and it happened years ago.

Yet who would trust a doctor bearing such a headline: KILLER MD FOUND.

Cary once described the real cost of becoming a Christian. Not *making* the declaration, but then feeling compelled to be more honest and caring. Which might be my real fear: that trusting Gerri with the truth would lead to our deeper relationship—or the execution chamber of my nightmare?

I risked it.

"When I was a kid I loved reading about the scrapes people got into," I said. "The local paper's column told of kids being arrested for shooting a pea shooter. They called it 'third degree assault.'"

"What's a pea shooter?"

"That's a colloquial phrase. It's a straw through which you blow something. Originally it was a pea but it could be anything. You're making me feel old—kids today carry guns. I was too innocent until I was thirty six. Before that the only time my name was in the papers was when I graduated from medical school. Just one of hundreds."

I stopped speaking, knowing that if I continued she would want to know everything.

"What happened then?" Gerri leaned forward.

I suddenly felt overwhelmed by guilt and wanted for Gerri to say that I was OK. So I told her.

"I once worked for the government. The job market for psychiatrists is never as good as for other doctors. Mental health is looked down on except when a crisis happens in *their* family. Then people can't get an appointment soon enough.

"And I was always considered old fashioned: being interested in why people did what they did, and doubtful about how helpful drugs really were. I'm not at all a typical psychiatrist."

"Which is another reason why I love you," she said, and I felt right in telling her.

"I love you too but don't interrupt my story—it's hard enough telling it."

"As bad as interrupting your jokes?"

"Much worse. This is serious stuff."

Gerri stroked my cheek. It wasn't easy accepting warmth—I was usually the one to supply it. I wanted to stop but I knew that she had a right to know before trusting me more with her children.

"You can imagine that with my attitudes I had trouble getting a job. I was repeatedly turned down except by those hospitals where they keep patients until their insurance runs out.

"I owed ninety eight thousand in student loans I wouldn't let my parents pay—this is another example of my not wanting to feel obligated.

"I was tired of driving a car with a broken muffler and working night/weekend shifts covering for doctors at a fifth of the money which they made. I wanted a job with regular hours. To be able to decide on a Friday that I needed a long weekend and feel comfortable about calling in sick. Laze away for forty hours a week instead of working seventy. So I looked for a job with the government, where I wouldn't be pressured to commit fraud. That's not too much to ask, is it? Just wanting to be an honest worker.

"Finally I saw an ad with only a box number. They wanted psychiatrists to evaluate workers. It's straightforward, worry-free work. You talk to someone and then write a report. So I sent in my resume and two months later I started working a forty hour week: evaluating employees who needed high security clearances or treatment during crises. Most were ordinary people except for some with the three letter agencies: CIA, DEA, NSA.

"Not many people want jobs which involve deceit so those agencies often hire people who *look* normal but have hidden impulses which are capable of being molded. Their freedom to act violently appealed to me. Maybe I want to do their work but am too controlled."

Gerri had stared silently but then spoke.

"You're so gentle with me and the kids. You'd never be like them," she said, as she massaged my neck.

Now I again feared that our relationship couldn't survive the truth but I continued speaking.

"I stopped buying newspapers after reading in the newspapers of why soldiers were being sent to Grenada— but earlier having learned the real reason from someone I evaluated. Later I learned of people being shot and apartments bombed. This didn't bother me since they were evil. I don't believe in God but know that devils exist and the world is better off without them."

"You're very moral."

"I like for justice to happen even with the mistakes that can sometimes get made achieving it.

"Afterwards they gave me two months leave and said that I should get away. I didn't know where to go but someone told me he could always recharge himself in rural Scotland. So I got the next flight and wandered its northeast: Portnockie and Findochty and Buckie. Places I never heard of or was back to again. Eating venison and grouse; even cranachan which is oatmeal and raspberries and cream. It was a different life."

"You went off your low-fat diet."

"It was a different life," I repeated.

"When I came back everyone was nice but I knew that I couldn't stay on that job. I had to start a new life where no one knew what I had done. Where I could escape my guilt."

Gerri then asked the question which I dreaded answering: "What did you *do*?"

I opened my mouth to reply but no words came out. So I drank more coffee and then I told her.

I told her even though I knew that it was a mistake to trust any woman.

I told her even though I needed her desperately and would never see her again once she learned my secret.

I told her because I felt that I had to confess—at that moment.

"I killed a woman," I said.

CHAPTER TEN

GERRI JUST STARED. Her look made me afraid to take her hand so I quickly began speaking.

"Because helping kids was always my first love, I worked evenings at a children's clinic which closed at seven when the guard left.

"I was treating a seven year old who was in foster care. His mother only saw him on Tuesdays at five, to take him out to eat for their weekly visit.

"One night she didn't come until everyone except us were gone. She was 'high,' babbling about evil and wanting to kill herself and her son—with the sawed-off shotgun under her raincoat which she suddenly pointed.

"I pushed him in back of me and said that people who want themselves dead feel unworthy of life. That change was always possible, and suicide was always a mistake.

"I seemed to be reaching her for her gun had drifted downwards. But then she screamed, 'it's time.' While I spoke I had been walking slowly towards her. I tried to keep her from pulling the trigger but as we struggled for the gun it went off and her face was blown away.

"I took the boy to another room and called the police. The first policeman who saw the body vomited.

"Though the inquest called the death 'suicide,' I left the clinic. The staff felt uncomfortable being around me: some said that I should have talked differently to her or not tried to take the gun.

They were scared that it might have happened to them and frightened doctors can be very critical. But the FBI liaisons at my day job understood and talking to them helped me.

"The first newspaper stories called me a hero: I had risked my life for a child. Later, some called it murder and demanded a state investigation. The mother was Black and Chicago race relations were tense. Medical Boards have wide leeway, an election was coming up, and some candidates needed headlines.

"After I came back from Scotland I was offered other government jobs in Washington and Pittsburgh but I wanted to be with people who didn't know what happened. So I started working about the country at temporary jobs, a traveling doctor. I was always afraid that someone would find out. I returned to New York City eleven years ago. That's it."

Gerri peeled my hand off the cup of coffee I held, caressed and kissed it.

"You saved a boy's life—not killed her!"

"My finger was by hers with the barrel pointed at her head. I know that you're right but I still ask myself whether I should have called Social Services when she didn't arrive on time. If I had dropped her son off with them maybe she'd still be alive."

"You'll kill yourself with 'maybes.' Maybe if I were short you wouldn't be interested in me."

"You think you know me so well," I said, feeling less gloomy. Still, I knew that when someone did something horrible people will shrink away from them—eventually.

A CIA psychiatrist I knew once witnessed an execution and never thought of it again. But thirty years later he still lobbied against capital punishment, it having affected him without his awareness. 'The unconscious is very powerful," he told me while dying.

But for now Gerri and I were still together. Though I didn't yet dare to tell her of my nightmare.

CHAPTER ELEVEN

I LEFT FOR work at ten, feeling relaxed and looking forward to the evening. My good mood remained until the phone rang, while I was eating my usual healthy lunch of re-heated tuna and rice.

"Hi—it's Joan."

"Joan..."

"*Carol's friend.*"

"Right. How are you? How's she?"

"One is now married. Which do you think?"

"Carol."

"How do you know?"

"I have a good effect on women. After dating me they decide, 'no more creeps,' and marry the next halfway decent guy they meet."

"You're still putting yourself down. I heard that you're living with someone. How is it going?"

"The kids, her, or me?"

"All together."

"Better than OK. Are you still with Hank?"

"Off and on." Then she came to the point. "I saw your photo on a desk during plea bargaining. Are you consulting for the DA?"

"No."

"It didn't look like that."

"What did it look like?"

"That you were a suspect."

"I may be suspected of being crazy but those people get rich not indicted."

"OK. But if you need help, we're friends. And I'm a very good lawyer."

We hung up, promising to get together.

I never treated political figures until The General came. Like with rabbis, they want a doctor who moves in the same cultural circles though he called me because he believed that we didn't.

The General continued telling stories and giving advice as he became more comfortable with me.

"Having power in Washington means being able to influence those who do and is the defining characteristic. Most political battles are won not from strength but from loss of confidence in others and the ensuing rush to cover.

"So one should never threaten to resign for this tells allies that you might abandon the issue. Nor should you accept what 'all the experts' say—they can be wrong, careless, or motivated for their own ends. You always need to get others on your side and in Washington the president is best."

"You sound cynical," I said.

"The first thing I would do at every new post was to adopt the commander's attitudes. If he was 'right wing' I'd agree that things were better during my father's days at West Point. I'd do his dirty work and keep my mouth shut. Becoming trusted, just like at a civilian job."

Yes, I thought, leading a deceitful life could lead to success. I *was* open but only with kids, which the General didn't have in his life.

"Life in Washington was the worst. Apparent good friends would change jobs and then you would get just yearly cards. Why did they bother with that? Because they might need you again.

"The more frequent their cards, the greater was their fear of what you might do with their secrets or write after retiring. How much do you tell? People can be dangerous when they feel threatened. Why risk anything?"

"You want to be honest with yourself," I suggested. "To know—completely—who you are."

He paused before speaking, now with increased emotion in contrast to the instructional tone he had been using.

"I've seen adult tantrums and drunken rages," he smiled slightly. "Politics can make very smart people act foolish. Maybe I was never meant for that life."

"How did you get to Washington?"

"My father wanted a closer family and pulled strings. That was what he was best at."

"What was your mother like?"

"She died from complications of diabetes after childbirth. My sister never married. It's the end of our line when we're gone."

There are different silences during therapy. "Bad," when the doctor must bridge the gulf separating him from the patient. "Good," when the patient is deciding whether to reveal a painful event or is growing emotionally.

This silence was a good one for I felt that I was starting to know The General. Not as one who is a presidential advisor but a man approaching the end of his life and still wondering who he really was.

The phone rang.

It was Paul Ascenci, my accountant/tax lawyer who previously spent years working for international firms. During his wife's unsuccessful battle against breast cancer he read medical books avidly. Later, being unable to travel while caring for their children, he developed a lucrative practice filing doctor's tax returns and representing them at hearings.

He often shared his medical opinions, behavior which they tolerated for they depended on him to guide their messy finances. And, often, he knew more about an ailment than they did. More than one of them said, "The best doctor I know does taxes."

"I know that you're busy and will be just a minute. Your federal returns for the past three years are being audited. If you haven't heard it's probably in today's mail."

"Should I worry?"

"I wouldn't. They probably got you mixed up with the Yungs from Hong Kong who became US citizens a few years ago. You should take my advice. Companies who did rarely paid taxes."

"I do. You're the best CPA and maybe even doctor I that know but I'm a worrier. How are your kids?"

"Giving me gray hairs. They think it's funny warning my dates to practice safe sex, but I'm getting emotionally freer."

"That *should* happen when parenting teens: learning from each other. I have to go. Thanks, I'll check my mail."

"Trouble?" Harold asked.

"Maybe my car was blocking a tax agent's driveway and he checked the plate. Bureaucrats have too much power—which you're the expert on. When did you retire?"

"Seven years ago next March. After being in nearly every state and country and visiting people who I first met at the War College: ex-Secretaries of State, Defense. They opened my eyes and made me want to participate in world events. But from the shadows, where it's safest."

It was time to end the session so I made my usual remark and went home.

The kids had eaten and were watching TV in their room. Gerri was opening wine and re-heating fish stew. Kirsten ran to be hugged, Karen watching briefly before leaving. I kissed Gerri on the cheek.

"I'm not three," she said. I kissed her on the lips.

"I know a lot about babies," Kirsten said, with great certainty.

"How do you know so much?" I asked.

"I listen to grown-ups," she replied solemnly.

"I wouldn't bet against her," Gerri said.

"What?" Kirsten asked.

"I'm just saying that you're a very smart little girl," Gerri told her.

Kirsten smiled slightly and returned to tussling with her sister over the TV's remote control.

Gerri had set up dinner on a folding table in the living room, the kitchen being so small. Apart from breakfast we ate together only Saturday evening and Sunday. Not like the fifties' *Ozzie And Harriet* TV series but a typical current lifestyle, with parents and children each having their own harried lives.

"Good," I said.

"Beats rice and tuna, huh?"

"We poor psychiatrists. Patients rage at us. Insurance companies don't pay. Women criticize our food. It's high in protein and low in fat. What's wrong with it?"

"That's not what I meant."

"You wonder how I survived without you."

"Something like that."

"So do I."

"That's better. You're learning. How was your day."

"Busy, but OK. Yours?"

"I mailed out two proposals but I'm not optimistic. Maybe I'm making excuses but I think that it would be easier if I were younger and wore pants. You got a letter. I put it on the bed so the kids wouldn't get it."

It read as Paul said: my tax returns were being audited in two weeks and I or a representative could appear. I'd let him go.

"Bad news?"

"My tax returns are being audited. I just wonder why for the past three years and not just one. My income didn't change much."

"Also, there's a package in the closet. It's been downstairs for at least a month—until the doorman remembered that you live here."

The box was about four by nine inches. Tape surrounded all of the edges. There was no return address but I knew who sent it. I shook it—nothing rattled. Then I squeezed it.

"You *are* nervous today. Do you want me to open it?"

"I'll do it. Go and watch TV with the kids for awhile."

"Are you *serious*? If it's dangerous, call the police—they're paid to take risks."

"I'm probably just being over-dramatic. Please humor me."

Gerri sighed. She was likely thinking: *Another Siggie. Why do I meet only 'nuts' like him?*

I tried to gently lift the tape but it was too well sealed. Frustrated, I abruptly tore the package open. Inside was a blue/green tie from Sulka.

I went to the girls' room.

"It's nothing."

"There's still a bomb shelter in the basement. Maybe you should get your meals and mail there!"

"I'm really sorry. At least now you know that I care."

"I'm glad you could express it so well!"

Gerri was really angry and I knew that if I didn't explain I risked being thrown out of the apartment that night.

I held her tightly. She looked away as I kissed her hair.

"I really was dumb. It won't happen again. Let me tell you about it," I said, placing my arm around her and forcing her to sit beside me on the sofa.

"I once treated a young woman," I said.

CHAPTER TWELVE

"Just like you're treating me," Gerri said, looking down but not moving away.

"Listen!" I pleaded, keeping my arm firmly about her. "She was a past patient, not girlfriend. I treated Louise for five years. She had big problems but looked more than OK—tall, with red hair and striking blue eyes. If you met her you'd be sure that she was normal."

"I'm not sure about anything now."

"Please. I hurt you and will try never to again. Let me finish." She caught her breath as I continued speaking.

"Louise got better but would still argue or 'accidentally' forget something on every job and quickly get fired. Finally she managed to keep one—until a manager touched her. The more she ignored him the worse it got. She complained and three months later she was laid off. This was a shock from which she never recovered.

"I prescribed tranquilizers, and once had her hospitalized her overnight. I tell patients to call me whenever they feel the need and knowing that they can is usually enough to keep them calm until their next appointment. But they rarely call except to re-schedule their appointment.

"It wasn't like that with Louise. We talked every night on the phone until I decided that maybe this was making her too dependent on me and stopped it.

"Which might have been a mistake, like encouraging her to make the job complaint. Or it could be that nothing could prevent what happened, which was that she started acting *really* crazy.

"Finally I said that therapy is just part of one's life: she needed the structure of a job or day hospital program too."

I held Gerri tightly, and felt like I was babbling though I sounded coherent. I was afraid. I knew that she would throw me out of her apartment the day she believed that I didn't care for her or was back at my usual scouting for women or dating several simultaneously.

"Louise wouldn't do either and I stopped treating her. Not immediately for it wouldn't have worked. She would still come to my office. But something she did caused her to be hospitalized by the police. Upon her release I agreed to treat her again but only if she would first stay in a program for three months. I probably sensed that she couldn't and didn't want to see her anymore. She was too much trouble.

"Now she drifts from one clinic to another. She sometimes stalks me, walking a half-block behind me until I go into a building. Or she'll get on the same bus but not talk to me.

"Sometimes she writes. I once answered and she wrote back that my letter upset her. Some people refuse to be helped. She hates herself for what she didn't achieve though people do the best that they can. A person's behavior sums up all of their conflicts and she's got a lot of them."

Gerri then spoke. "You could call it her vector—a math term which summarizes quantity and direction."

"How do you know that?"

"My degree was in math."

"I didn't know."

"You don't know a lot. Which is why you need me to teach you."

Then I knew that we were still OK and started to relax but I felt she had to know a little more.

"She's still angry and makes me nervous, even if she'd never harm me. I'm sorry that telling you this took so long."

"Do you realize how often you apologize? Everyone makes mistakes."

"A doctor shouldn't."

"But you're my lover and I'll still love you even when you do."

I didn't reply as most men would: that I loved her too. But I had never used this word seriously and still couldn't. Maybe Gerri sensed this for she didn't remark on it.

The girls, half-asleep and staring at the TV, protested only mildly as we carried them to their beds. Ordinarily I would have worried about the IRS letter and Joan's call. Now I only thought what to cook for their breakfast and of silly comments which they might enjoy.

Later in bed, as I closed my eyes, I again began to fear that my electric chair nightmare would occur, I considered the mother's death in Chicago—the woman I felt that I killed. Could *this* explain the dream? I was hopeful—until I remembered that the dream had begun thirty one years earlier.

Gerri was right. My frequent apologies *were* odd. Did they derive from the doctors' creed of not tolerating mistakes—or simple guilt?

But all my anxiety disappeared as we lay spoon fashion, with my penis hardening. In the past when feeling erotic I woke Gerri. Now I just held her tighter and tried to match my breathing to hers. There were fewer emotional highs and lows when living a coupled life and I hoped for another night of untroubled sleep.

My mind drifted to an eight year old boy's play therapy session that day and the fantasy he created.

"Let's kidnap the school bus. Then take off the girls' clothes and torture 'em," he said.

"I ain't gonna do that," I responded vehemently, "That's naughty." Then, softly, "Why do you want to torture them?"

"We don't have to," he quickly replied, catching himself. Feeling uneasy at having revealed his unconscious impulses. From this trim, courteous boy. Who so resembled his proper doctor.

CHAPTER THIRTEEN

My nightmare didn't return but my stomach still rumbled. It felt like it does before getting married (as people have told me); or when a patient is deteriorating and a doctor must make rapid decisions.

Though the morning had seemed ordinary. The kids insisted that I drink from a sippy cup since only babies would make pancakes without blueberries, which I had inadvertently done. I hoped that they wouldn't demand this from me for too long.

Despite my long experience with kids some parenting duties did terrify me. I'm what psychiatrists call anal, which means being overly concerned with order and cleanliness. This disappears from most parents after their first child but it might not have changed me. A patient who had vomited following her first diapering concluded that she wasn't made to be a parent. "Right on!" I would have agreed if I wasn't treating her.

But I did learn: how difficult kids can be and angry a parent then becomes; what clothing goes together, and how to braid hair. Slowly, I did change.

I brushed and braided Kirsten's and Karen's hair and helped to select their clothes. But I also thought up plausible reasons why I shouldn't aid with their toileting. Like I said, I'm anal.

It's only partly true that doctors become psychiatrists because of their interest in behavior. Many also can't stand the sight of blood and you know what else.

Gerri was up since five, writing and phoning Denmark before the charges went up. Until leaving for university she lived at Torshavn, the capital of the Danish Faroe Islands. Her mother was a science teacher, and her father was a government bureaucrat. I didn't know why her childhood was so unhappy and told myself that she wasn't my patient and would reveal more when she was ready. Which she soon did.

She spoke of having starved herself when she was thirteen, lying in bed and hearing the doctor say that she would die. She then opened her eyes and began eating again.

A year later she met a much older, equally scarred man who was vacationing in Faeröerne (as the region is spelled in Danish). He was recovering from injuries which he suffered during World War Two. Though initially they were only friends, a relationship which her parents viewed as being "sweet," they became lovers when she turned sixteen. Their affair lasted until she was well enough to begin school on the mainland.

And that's all I knew about her. Plus that I was now her only lover and the one she would entrust her children to were she to die. I suddenly got nervous after she suggested this and, considering her excellent health, considered her concern as being morbid. Later I realized she was just being more grown up than me.

Gerri's parents didn't often visit or send presents. But "Uncle Maurice" made up for this with his gifts in the fall and spring. Kirsten's were more elaborate than Karen's. Apparently Maurice preferred traditional feminine behavior over independence.

So despite my worries a lot of good things were happening in my life. What most men experience when they were much younger but I was first getting around to.

Like learning the deep emotions which commitment to a relationship arouses and which children can generate. And letting it be OK to feel inadequate after—blamelessly—disappointing a child. Still, something unsettling happened every day, these events being caused by the friction which was aroused by our unique personalities slowly meshing.

That day, after leaving the apartment, I bought *The New York Times* and *Wall Street Journal* as I had begun doing. Then I waited for the buses at the same corners, again failed to get a seat, and met Rev. Cary outside my office door. We went in and I offered him coffee. He accepted this for the first time, which was another indicator of his increasing comfort with therapy.

"You're a better doctor than coffee maker," he said after a sip.

"I do my best with both."

"So...how long do I have to come?"

"Another put-down. I'm starting to think that you don't like being here," I said, smiling slightly to show that I was aware of his true feelings.

"That's a good question: how long therapy lasts depends. A patient might relocate, or have made as much change as they can then tolerate in their life."

"What about me?"

"I don't yet know. You're very bright but despite this did manage to mess up your career. My job is to make this less likely in the future, not turn you into my clone. I wouldn't wish this on anyone." I also mellowed this statement with a smile.

We both became silent. Not a comfortable or uncomfortable one. A thoughtful pause.

"What if I assured you that I'd never touch another parishioner?"

"I would believe you even if I don't understand why it happened. Which means that I'm sensing you don't either and why it *might* happen again. But therapy is just for a period of time. Not till the doctor's mortgage gets paid."

This bad joke usually aroused a smile. It didn't then.

"How does *murdering* a woman compare with loving her?" Cary asked angrily.

CHAPTER FOURTEEN

THOUGH HE WAS two inches taller and forty pounds heavier, I thought of strangling Cary. Then I wondered *why* his question had so enraged me. I said that he didn't have good self-control and he became angry—like anyone would. So replied with something hurtful to make me feel just as bad.

And his statement surprised me only because I had tried to forget the mother's death for so long. Gerri was the only person I told of it though others could easily find out— even if eleven years past was now considered a century ago.

I also realized that for Cary to speak so openly meant that he trusted me, and sensed that I wouldn't deliberately hurt him.

Yet something still nagged at me. Until I remembered an incident from when I worked as chief psychiatric resident in a large city hospital while the nurses struck. Most of the doctors went into work for we were threatened with bad job recommendations and complaints to the state licensing board otherwise.

During a class I was teaching on psychiatric diagnosis, an intern asked what the psychology of a doctor was who actively opposed his colleagues as they tried to improve the job conditions for all of them.

My hands quickly swept towards his neck—until I regained control and said that I wouldn't discuss this issue and our discussion returned to mental health matters.

It was only later that I realized my rage had come from he having baited me as my mother did years before. And that this hadn't been my first impulse to kill.

Turning away from my personal issues, I needed to discover what really bothered Cary.

"What's on your mind?"

"Dissembler. A purveyor of truths about others. How many have you murdered?"

"Look...*if* something about my life is relevant to your therapy I'll certainly discuss it. What are you referring to?"

"The death in Chicago," he said. Now so calmly that I immediately concluded that his earlier anger had arisen from his disappointment at the surprising information he learned. "A crazy mother tried to shoot her child. While you shielded him and struggled for the gun she was killed."

"Did you read the grand jury transcript which they voted to release."

"Yes."

"What did you feel?"

"I envied you."

Cary's response amazed me. "Why?"

"You were Christlike—as I would like to be."

"Oh, come on!" I exclaimed. Feeling more unsettled by his use of religious symbolism than if he asserted I had copulated with an extraterrestrial, or her brother.

But Cary didn't intend to be complimentary and was concerned with his spiritual anguish.

85

"I'm serious. While I attended Union Theological Seminary I dressed like a studied cleric but didn't sense myself to be really Christian and felt a fraud. So the others went to parishes and I chose Vietnam. Not as soldier, but there's still a big difference between helping twenty year olds die and running mothers' meetings.

"Then I realized that the only way to become a real Christian—Christlike—was *to be like Him*. Slough off self-centeredness and jealousy. Like someone who's shy starting to act friendly and then becoming so.

"At first I thought myself delusional. People thinking they're Him wind up in mental hospitals. But then it made sense: that to become Christlike one had to strive to be good beyond goodness and accepting beyond acceptance. Phrases without literal sense but they are not meant to be considered intellectually.

"And it worked. My behavior became less pretense and I injected my change into others, seeking for them *to become* too. Like a portrait being painted slowly appears. Then I felt calm, for with Christ beside me, I was no longer alone."

Wow, I thought. If I spoke like this to Gerri, a fellow unbeliever, she would ask if I was coming down with the flu.

None of the clerics I treated had spoken this way. They referred to "personal problems" and "stress," concepts which I related to easily. But Cary must sense that I could respond to his experience too. But isn't every doctor Christlike? I asked myself, having always believed that my work reflected my most commendable personal characteristics.

86

Feeling the need to return to firmer ground, I turned our discussion to concrete details.

"What was your wife educated in?"

"Accounting, when she decided on a business career. Before that she was trained as a nurse. That was when we both wanted to heal: she, the body, I, the spirit. It was an imperfect match."

"How so?"

"Healing the body is easier. The soul is messy. You should be able to understand that."

I ignored his sarcasm. This was caused by his anxiety at having revealed himself.

"Why did you marry her?"

"We were theologically compatible. Seeking that union which Christianity postulates as being humanity's ideal goal. But we probably never could achieve this together."

"Why not?"

"We're too different. But she's a good clergyman's wife: there has never been a scandal or troublesome kids. Maybe I shouldn't be so critical—she hasn't had an easy time with me."

"When did your other relationships start?"

"What relationships?"

I didn't pressure him for Cary had to speak voluntarily—if he intended to remain ordained. So I gazed at the cabinet beside him, then out the window at the clouds. Waiting. And eventually he did speak.

"At my first parish. She was twenty one and pregnant. Her boyfriend was a loser who spent his money on his car. 'The least you could do is buy me underwear,' she told him, and demanded that he grow up. 'We're not kids anymore—we're having a baby together.'"

"The heavier she became the more radiant she appeared to me: hers was a holy mission, to merge her life with her child's and theirs with the father.

"She had no one: her mother drank and usually wasn't home; her father lived across the country. At first she came to church weekly, then daily. Sometimes we spoke but mostly I listened. Then I found myself worrying about her at night. I got her a job in the meal program to be sure that she ate enough. Which I insisted on, like a father though I wasn't that much older. But no one who had been in Vietnam was ever young again.

"She broke up with her boyfriend and the last I heard she was going into labor."

It seemed a good time to stop so I said my usual and he quietly left the office. The day was young but I was already worn out: from the memory he aroused, the IRS tax hassle, and my sense of impending crisis though not what it was about.

CHAPTER FIFTEEN

Hours later I welcomed The General's appearance for it marked the end of my workday.

His and Cary's treatments were contrasts. My goal for Cary was to reduce his likelihood of behaving improperly. I didn't yet know The General's.

I thought to start by learning how he spent his days but didn't want to seem intrusive: he was still completely comfortable only when telling shopworn stories. So I began indirectly, by telling one of mine.

"I once had an office next to a government agency which got jobs for people who still wanted to work though being in their sixties, seventies, even eighties. One had been wthe as manager for a huge American company. He was never sick during the forty three years at his job but two months after retiring he wound up in a hospital. I always felt that it was a mistake for people to stop working suddenly. How do you spend your time?"

When Harold replied, it wasn't another unrevealing story.

"My friends are in Washington. I'm alone a lot but not uncomfortable. I read, and people call me for advice, which I'm glad to give. What else can guys my age do except to tell what they've learned. I also plan conferences."

"For which group?"

"The University War Study Circle. Despite the name, it's not secret. It's been around for forty years and is funded with foundation money and a little from the government.

"The members are academicians or from the military or intelligence. They publish a journal which covers everything from a history of flogging in the navy to the limits of nuclear deterrence for Israeli security."

"It sounds like a full-time job."

He shrugged. "I always juggled two or three."

"Did you ever consider marriage?"

"I thought about it, but closeness can be so hard to achieve after some childhoods that it's almost miraculous when it occurs. But I've done lots of things and you can't have everything. I've been to funerals of much younger people, kids really. Even in peacetime there are foul-ups. Which is something you don't know unless you're in the military—all the funerals you attend."

A few minutes later his session was over and I puttered at the desk as the phone rang.

"You're talking to another woman!"

An understandable statement from Gerri considering my past, though her tone was joking.

"You're the only one for me."

"*This* month."

"*Every* month. What's for dinner."

"A special I'm slaving over. The kids want to talk."

"Luv ya," Kirsten whispered. "Karen wanted to talk too but left," Gerri added. Karen was more reserved than her sister.

"Luv you too. Be home soon," I said to Kirsten, feeling, finally, that I had found a home.

To my surprise, as I entered the waiting room to leave, I found two men dressed in what I used to call "Sears suits" before their brand became indistinguishable from more expensive ones to the untrained eye.

Both were above six feet. One was heavy with thinning red hair and prominent blood vessels in his nose; the younger was black and athletic. They arose as I entered the room.

"Dr. Yungg? Dr. Lewis Yungg?" the older man asked.

After I affirmed this, his response surprised me, yet seemed to be one which I had been waiting for all of my life.

"We have a warrant for your arrest. For murder," he said.

CHAPTER SIXTEEN

TREATING POLICE OFFICERS had never made me nervous, but then *I* was in control. So I wound up making the the usual statement: that they had the wrong person. Were they *sure* they wanted me?

We all remained polite in this drama which I experienced as surrealistic, despite my long expectation.

They said we had to leave and that I could call Gerri from the station house. Using this phrase rather than "jail." Like doctors who, having been made gun-shy by patients' emotional outbursts, thereafter describe cancer as being "a growth."

And, yes, they apologized, they did have to handcuff me—but with my coat over my hands no one would notice.

I submitted. What choice did I have? I wrote a note stating that I had been called away and for patients to call to reschedule their appointments. Which the black detective obediently fastened to the door during our distasteful situation.

Then I calmed down and remembered the advice which I often gave to teenagers, who had the most frequent contact of all my patients with the police.

"Talk only to your lawyer. Never accept anything from the police. Not even a soda."

I determined to follow this, having treated adolescents who, after being lulled by a policeman's helpful attitude, thereafter spoke freely with their statement becoming the only evidence against them.

All of which was easier said than done.

During our ride one detective joked that I was the first psychiatrist he ever arrested. I responded that crime couldn't be under control with so few doctors in jail. His reply, that the Corrections Department couldn't afford to hire a shrink and so they had to arrest one, caused my position to sink in.

I hadn't read the warrant closely, then being too upset to channel my anxiety into constructive thinking. Though having been a solitary doctor, I sensed that being a similar prisoner would doom me. I needed friends; most of all, I needed a lawyer.

As I watched passersby through the car window, I wanted to shield my face and wondered how much reporters would want to know about me—probably everything.

News of the mother's death would certainly be dredged up. Thankfully, I had already told Gerri—who *might* stand by me. But would her children, after they received the playground comment "Your daddy's a killer!"?

The car became enmeshed in traffic. I expected the detective to use the siren. Then I thought that maybe he enjoyed my company and felt happy at being able to please him. Until I recognized that, just minutes after my arrest, I had begun to suffer from the Stockholm Syndrome, which caused prisoners to identify with the interests of their captors.

So I silently vowed to act three roles: the obedient, observant prisoner who used his medical knowledge for favors, which were the equivalent of fees in the society I was entering; the dignified professional who healed not destroyed life; *and* the organizer of my defense. I couldn't wholly trust any lawyer whose major interest was their fee.

As the car stopped, my thinking ended. Some was repetitive but I felt that my salvation lay in letting it ramble. I had faith in its underlying logic, which likely was lacking in the world I was entering.

What happened initially was as I expected. I stood at a desk and emptied my pockets in exchange for a receipt. Then I was asked if I wanted to use the toilet and later, despite my warning to teenagers, accepted coffee and a cheese sandwich.

After refusing to speak with a detective without my attorney present, I was offered three calls ("usually just one, doctors get three"). I dreaded having to inform Gerri of my situation, so soon after she learned of the mother's death and Louise.

Next must be my call to a criminal defense lawyer. Maybe even the late John Gotti's for who knew what evidence the police had.

This apparently random thought (talk about help from the unconscious!) reminded me that I did know someone who could help. A year earlier I had treated the four year old daughter of an elderly mobster, Enrico (his fifty one years younger wife called him Henry). Her mother brought her after the child tried to smother her infant sister with a pillow.

I saw the mother and child (whose sister lay in a carry basket) five or six   times. And talk about being motivated for treatment: the older child once punched her mother in the face when it was time to leave.

By our last session this child was affectionate towards her sister and their mother was more assertive with her husband—who no longer threatened to break his older daughter's neck unless she behaved. I never met Enrico/Henry but at our last session I was told that he was grateful and would welcome helping me, though feeling that nothing he did could satisfy his debt to me.

I felt moved: psychiatrists are delighted just to have their bills paid and not get sued. I never, until now, considered taking up his offer.

Sensing that the policeman's courtesy wouldn't last, I told him Gerri's number. He dialed, then busied himself with paperwork and pretended not to listen. She picked up on the second ring.

"*Why aren't you home*? It's after nine. Do you *know* how long it takes to make salmon mousse with sour-cream dill sauce? You don't *want* to hear all the ingredients!"

Joan's name popped into my mind as I interrupted her—and wondered if I would ever again be consumed with such ordinary matters.

"Please just listen. I'm in jail and have been charged with murdering an ex-patient. It's nonsense but I need a lawyer and will tell you who to call. Don't worry. Everything will be all right."

I gave her Joan's name. Partly because she was the only lawyer that I knew but also because she had sensed that something was happening. Maybe also because women tend to be more empathic than men, something which I then needed almost as much as legal skill.

"Tell me what to do," Gerri said calmly.

"Her number is in the phone book. Tell who you are, that I've been arrested and am at the West Ninety Fifth Street precinct. Don't come—only she can help me now. I'll be with you soon. I have to hang up."

"OK. I love you."

I said that I loved her too and thought how sad it was that the first time I told a woman this—and meant it!—we couldn't be together.

"Next," I said to the officer.

"Only one call is permitted. I was joking about three," he smirked.

Reputable people no longer respected doctors, I thought. Seeking Enrico's aid began looking better.

CHAPTER SEVENTEEN

WHILE SITTING ALONE in a holding cell, I began adjusting to my surroundings. I became struck by the level of noise and activity.

I never liked groups, my only comparable one being the army which I joined following medical school in order to get my education loans paid. After commissioning, I was sent to North Carolina for socialization into military ways. There, to my amazement, I was described as being "a natural shot" by an old sergeant, though my talent was derided by the other doctors.

This ex-Bronx boy now found that he loved guns. Their odor and power, how efficiently they operated, even cleaning them. In short, I became a "gun nut" and spent many enjoyable hours talking with the sergeant in his armory office and drinking with him elsewhere. But like the other doctors I hated the boredom of military training.

It's painful for bright people not to think and often there wasn't much thinking required. Some doctors even hoped for an accident so they could do some real work, though not that it should happen to them mind you.

I'm big and look athletic, and have such a mean (or absent minded) expression that others apologize when *I* walk into *them*. But the only physical activity I'm interested in is sex and I never fought as a child.

So, disliking groups and needing intellectual stimulation, I concluded that I wasn't psychologically equipped for jail. I didn't yet feel afraid though maybe this was only because my real situation had not yet sunk in. Self-protection must be my first priority.

Even I knew that a murder charge elevated my status above that of common inmate. If things got really bad, Enrico, likely, *could* protect me. But his interest would inevitably become known and not do my public image any good.

I imagined a possible headline: ACCUSED KILLER PSYCHIATRIST HAS SECRET MOBSTER BUDDY. DA WEIGHS SEARCH OF JERSEY LANDFILL FOR MORE VICTIMS.

What was as important as insuring my safety was discovering what happened to Louise and why I was the only suspect. I knew that doctors occasionally killed their spouse or lover but not, deliberately, patients. Then I remembered reading about some who did. Several doctors killed at least one person, and another murdered four, he then returning home to South America and never being charged. The author related these homicides to the doctors' early experiences with their mothers, a conclusion which, for some reason, fascinated me.

I got company: a short Hispanic man in his early thirties wearing a T-shirt emblazoned "Born Loser." This motto seemed appropriate for him until I warned myself that such condescension affected my survival.

He spoke first, and with greater fluency than I anticipated.

"There's not much class in here."

"That's the last thing on my mind."

"What're you in for?"

"Murder."

His slight move away didn't make me feel any better. He shook his head slightly, apparently having concluded, with a twist on the proverb, that it takes all kinds of people to fill a jail.

"What do you think my charge is," he challenged.

"Don't know."

"Child abuse—it's a lie."

"What does your lawyer say?"

"I haven't seen her yet."

"What happened?"

"My father's Russian, mother a Mexican, wife is Puerto Rican. 'Don't date a Spanish girl,' my mother always warned. 'They look easy but it's hard looking easy and only a real Spanish man can control them.'

"My wife left me after I pressured her to get a job. When my lawyer questioned her lover's drug use, she said that I molested our daughter."

This accusation didn't surprise me. Throughout the eighties, until public irrationality and anxiety subsided, I was amazed at the nonsensical "evidence" (nightmares, inattention in school, bed wetting) which caused reputable people to be convicted of child abuse, since these symptoms almost always reflect other causes.

I felt for my unknown cell mate. Maybe it was like this in jail, I thought. Where one made real friendships, strengthened by the shared anxiety of lives passing unlived. The harsh sound of metal onto metal pulled my thinking back to reality: we were getting company.

CHAPTER EIGHTEEN

HE WAS BIG AND smelled. He had dirty hair and ragged clothes with only his combat boots being cared for. A scar above his right eyebrow, the residue of having had his nose broken repeatedly, and his thickened knuckles added to his charm.

On his upper left arm was tinea versicolor, a contagious fungal infection which begins as a white patch then darkens, causing its Latin name meaning "many colored." An earring in his right ear made me think of a joke which even I wasn't stupid enough to tell. He didn't look like he had a sense of humor. He looked like a goon.

My nameless friend and I shared a brief glance.

The Goon sprawled on the bench, closed his eyes and farted. When he began snoring I smiled towards my new friend—as much as I could.

"Lew Yungg."

"Isaac Mendez-Solov," he quickly responded.

"Your mother was a modern woman," I said, referring to his hyphenated name.

"I should have followed her advice."

"Do you want more? I'm a psychiatrist who has testified in abuse cases."

Now he became cautious, possibly thinking that if The Goon was an obvious thug I could be a less apparent crazy.

"I can use all the advice I can get."

"OK. Try to remember that you're in New York City and not a small town. Here, judges know that most abuse charges by a divorcing parent are lies to get what they want. How old is your daughter?"

"Three."

"*No* prosecutor will take the case with a witness that young unless there's physical evidence so no need to rely on her testimony. Was there evidence? The tearing of skin or presence of venereal disease?"

"If there was, it wasn't from me!"

I would have felt better helping him had I received his assertive "no," but I needed friends and could fine-tune my ethics when my own legal mess was over.

"If there is evidence it could be the boyfriend's, and that your daughter was brainwashed. Police aren't good at interviewing kids. Have your lawyer get transcripts of their meetings. If your wife was present at any of them then the statements are worthless."

Now there was a comfortable silence, like during better therapy sessions.

"You *are* a psychiatrist."

"Until two hours ago. Now I'm a prisoner/doctor.

"What happened?"

"An ex-patient who I didn't treat in years was murdered. I don't know what evidence they have."

I felt uneasy at violating my rule that an arrested person speaks only to their lawyer but I didn't think he was a plant. And even psychiatrists need support sometimes.

"I wish I could help you—you gave me better advice than my parents. My father is a waiter but was a surgeon in the old Soviet Union. My mother sells clothes from the garment center and makes more than him. Sometimes he slaps her to show who's the boss."

I was right. He couldn't be a plant for his story was so odd that it must be true. Even the detail like his father hitting his mother, which is common with husbands from former Communist countries.

We became silent. I tried to relax but thoughts of my conviction and execution ran through my mind. Finally I dozed off, being awakened by the sound of three prisoners being led in: one Black, one Oriental, the third looking very Irish. All were expensively dressed, they possibly having been arrested at an expensive massage parlor after giving a seminar on the British government's attitude towards integration into the European Monetary Union.

But I never did learn who they really were for a minute later an officer entered and his voice pierced the noise.

"How many of you have been arrested before?"

The Goon, leisurely, raised his arm, "Yo." Isaac's response was slower.

The newcomers huddled as the policeman exhibited a look which seemed to say: just shows how poorly we do our jobs if so few like you have been arrested.

Then he continued. "There's a procedure we follow and the lieutenant will describe it. He's a lawyer. Retiring soon, so give him respect." The Goon made another "Yo."

I wondered whether the speech of his boss derived from a new "treat-prisoners-more-professionally" policy or because prosperous ones were more likely to sue if treated inappropriately, thus threatening lucrative pensions. Or maybe, like military dentists approaching discharge who only then ask patients to state when a procedure hurts, the lieutenant was practicing courtesy in his waning days of public service. It didn't matter to me: I could use any information.

The lieutenant arrived almost as if on cue. He was short, with carefully combed, wavy, black/gray hair, wire framed eyeglasses, and a heavily starched uniform. He likely felt as upset by The Goon's appearance as the rest of us.

Holding a pad with neatly numbered paragraphs, he began speaking.

"I won't say 'greetings' because I'm sure that you want to be here as little as I wish it. But we all have our prescribed roles, you as citizens and we as officers enforcing the peace."

He paused to let his words sink in. I was impressed and immediately felt less hopeless. This was probably what he wanted since desperate prisoners cause problems.

"Booking a person," the lieutenant continued, "is an informal procedure which is not required by law. It consists of preparing a card with the name of the prisoner, their alleged crime, the time of their arrest and more. *Record-keeping,* since each of you now has a record which will account for you until you appear before a magistrate. This also permits relatives to learn of your arrest. It's boring and I apologize. But with our new equipment, fingerprinting is no longer a filthy experience."

This really is a new type of police officer, I thought, as his subordinate looked gloomy.

The oriental man nodded, indicating a question.

The lieutenant looked pleased. "How can I help you?"

"Is it necessary that people be able to learn of our arrest?"

"I'm sorry but the records are public for your protection. Though big city newspapers don't have such listings so no one should learn of it. We've all done things which we'd prefer for others not to learn. Isn't that so, Officer Zerofelli?"

Zerofelli agreed, and likely prayed daily for the quicker retirement of his boss if my experience treating police officers provided an accurate guide to their attitude.

The Irishman now spoke with a French accent, and I noted that my conclusions about people weren't being too accurate today.

"How can I help?" the lieutenant repeated.

"How long will we be here?"

The lieutenant smiled again. "What's wrong with my new jail?" Then he became serious.

"Probably just overnight unless you're not released on bail, Rikers Island is crowded, or a special service is needed which it takes time to arrange. We're a way-station.

"I've told you this so you know that there's a purpose for everything we ask you to do. With your cooperation we can fulfill these quickly. You may not leave recommending us to your friends (said with a small smile) or mail us a thank you note (another smile), but you *will* respect our professionalism. Wouldn't you agree, Officer?"

Zerofelli continued playing his part.

"Right, sir."

"Officer Zerofelli will now aid you with booking. If hungry or wishing to wash, your needs will be met so you can look and feel your best in court. The best of luck to you all!"

The lieutenant smiled again and exited our stage, or so it seemed. I was sorry to see him go, feeling safer when he was with us. Which wasn't my imagination.

Now Zerofelli spoke.

"The lieutenant is a lawyer. My job is to tell you what to do and how to do it. If you don't, we'll make you and other charges will be filed. Food comes after booking. Anyone want to shit, we make a bathroom stop now—I don't want you smelling up our jail. Any questions?"

This time there were none. I felt as if the lieutenant was a million miles away, if he ever existed.

CHAPTER NINETEEN

IN TURN WE answered questions, were assigned numbers, and had our photos taken by computer. This was little different from the procedure when I purchased membership in a shopping club a week before. Despite its modern equipment the unhurried atmosphere still resembled that of jails in old black-and-white movies.

During these boring procedures my mind not unexpectedly turned to sex, and a twenty year old virgin nursing student I dated during medical school.

We met at a folk dance, ate at a cheap restaurant, then returned to my apartment. I guess she felt it was time for her to have sex since she didn't protest when I undressed her, she later saying, "I want you inside me again." I remember saying how good her surprisingly small vagina felt and she agreeing that it was small.

She objected to some sexual activities until, between our second and third dates, her sociology class was assigned a graphic book on intimate practices (don't ask me why). Then she insisted on showering together even when I was so tired that I could barely tramp from door to bed. And she became open to oral sex, though not letting me perform it on her. Maybe you can figure out why.

I should have married her despite my unease that she was an observant Catholic. I didn't then realize how much people can change after marriage. I was partial to Catholic girls later; and Mormons ever since I worked in Utah. Both groups seemed to particularly value commitment.

As I grew older, girlfriends questioned why I never married. Still, they accepted my plausible reasons: that I never met the "right" woman; was too career oriented; was taking longer than most men to grow up. Until my sudden disappearance confirmed that these "explanations" were lies.

The truth was that *I didn't know why*. I was a cautious guy and wondered whether I could be a good father since treating children is easier than parenting them —but many married men doubt this.

Or maybe I feared being dominated; which explains why I'm most comfortable with docile women like Gerri, who lets me make decisions. Even what preschool her children attend or when they go to sleep. I don't want to make these decisions since I'm not their father—yet. But maybe Gerri is trying to force me to realize that *I could be* a good parent, which she senses I question. This would make her very perceptive indeed and mean that someday, *maybe*, we *could* marry.

My thinking continued as we were marched to a small lunch room where I chose (one) turkey and processed Swiss cheese hero sandwich, (one) apple juice, and tea, while noting that even prisoners have some choices.

The building was new and more greatly resembled an expensive condominium than precinct. It had air conditioning, indirect lighting, a tree filled atrium, and a community room which neighborhood groups were encouraged to use, with the hope thereby of increasing public cooperation with the police. Then conflict arose, as always seems to happen with anything progressive in New York.

An Oklahoma based fundamentalist Christian group sought the meeting room to begin their campaign entitled "Reclaiming New York For Jesus."

Perhaps in response, a lesbian gathering requested it for their group to discuss how to use sex toys more effectively. They then released a video detailing their optimal use and I fantasized members dressed in police uniforms demonstrating them.

Which was all pretty funny and part of that madness which makes the City attractive to foreigners who consider American sexual prudery to be hilarious.

The predictable happened: permission to use the room was refused for both groups who then sued. Ideally they would have cooperated but they didn't, and the court finally ruled that all or no groups could use the room.

The ensuing cancellation disappointed many for the video was the talk of the neighborhood and would likely have permanently cemented community/police relations. Maybe arousing dinner invitations for officers—with or without their dildoes. And if the two groups of speakers met back to back they would engender such a crowd as to give the lie to those who describe New York City as godless.

Now, seated in my stainless steel/concrete cell, I felt free from personal responsibilities as only those whose decisions are made for them can. And I had no more thinking. Until Isaac, seated on the bunk above, asked, "What would you do if you were me?"

CHAPTER TWENTY

I THOUGHT FOR several moments. Not to seem like the popular image of a psychiatrist but because answering his question was complicated. As a potential ally it wasn't good to upset him but I couldn't think of anything to say which wouldn't. For Isaac to be arrested there must be *some* evidence. And he *might* have abused his daughter even if apparently identical behaviors may or may not amount to it.

A father with lustful thoughts while drying his four year old's pubic area after her bath is committing abuse which is impossible to prosecute. Yet without these thoughts there wasn't any since he had no sexual motive. Sometimes it isn't easy to decide.

I relaxed, for no peer review panel would evaluate my advice and I needed his expertise too.

"Most importantly, I'd try to stay calm," I began. "Your problem isn't what happened but what a prosecutor can convince a grand jury of. Most will indict anyone but getting *a jury* to agree is harder, even when a prosecutor has a pliable expert witness. It's not proper to buy a doctor's testimony but every lawyer knows what their— expensive— witness will say. How well are you fixed?"

"My parents will help. They'll never see their granddaughter if I lose."

"Don't think like that."

I wanted to get Isaac's mind off the accusation. I knew that obsessing about what might happen could destroy you.

"What kind of work do you do?"

"Computer consultant."

I was impressed. Isaac could be valuable when I got out for my current one was a teenage neighbor.

"Where did you learn about computers?"

"From books, and in the Legion of Doom."

Another nut-case, I told myself, and couldn't have been more wrong.

"What's that?" I asked, hesitantly.

"Not what it sounds like. Just kids with made-up names playing games with things they didn't think were real. Cars are real, not credit card numbers on a computer. We became outlaws without leaving our bedrooms. An older friend became *the* Lex Luthor, its founder. He got famous. I was arrested for breaking into systems of companies which my mother bought from. They got suspicious after word got back about our super low prices. We paid up. It should have been more but they were embarrassed."

"So why were you arrested?"

"For being too good at 'social engineering.' I'd call Western Union and ask for a money advance on 'my' card.

"They'd verify my identity but I had already switched the card holder's number in their file to that of a local pay phone. Then I began ordering computers and business boomed. My parents thought technology was the wave of the future but I knew that crime paid better. After getting out of jail I worked in Internet security though my becoming reformed doesn't seem to have helped."

Then, both being talked out and worn out, we fell asleep. My electric chair nightmare didn't return.

CHAPTER TWENTY ONE

I was awakened by the sound of my name, and stood up to re-enter my living nightmare.

Wearing my jail issued slippers, I was escorted by the guard to a small room containing two plastic chairs and a circular Formica-topped metal based table. All of the furniture was bolted to the floor and identical to that over which I conducted psychiatric evaluations in the past. Joan smiled when she saw me but she didn't look happy.

"How are you?"

"What's up doc?"

"Always joking."

"It keeps me from going crazy."

"How bad was it?"

"Not much for a jail. Even the company was interesting. Maybe I should practice here and avoid office rent."

"It's never easy," she said, looking concerned. "I wanted information before coming. There wasn't anything I could do until then and I knew that you know enough not to talk."

Having gained the empathy I needed, I shifted my weight on the too small stool.

"What's this case about?"

Joan hesitated before speaking, as if she now needed to regard me in a new light. "You're *accused* of murdering an ex-patient, Louise Werziner. Her mutilated body was found, incompletely burned, in an abandoned building a mile from your apartment."

"Many things are a mile away from it."

"*With* a partially completed letter to her grandmother saying that if you didn't keep treating her she'd *tell everything*."

"Everything what?"

"It didn't say."

"Nothing happened that doesn't happen in therapy. We talked and I told her some bad jokes which she wasn't social enough to laugh at. I stopped her treatment when she started acting *too* crazy."

"There's more."

"They found my confession."

"It's almost as bad. Her diary has lots of sex in it which relates to you. Who, she wrote, was meeting her the night before she disappeared. And she told her roommate of the meeting."

This nightmare was getting worse. What really scared me was that while psychiatrists know the kind of bizarre thinking which craziness can cause, laymen (which includes lawyers and judges) only *think* that they do. Sexual "smoke" in a patient's words are no evidence that there was sex with the doctor though I knew that it would be an uphill battle to convince a prosecutor of this.

"Any more?" I was starting to feel woozy.

115

"The club outside your door was custom made and traced to you. They're testing the blood stains and hair on its base."

"It's a *walking stick*. The umbrella stand holding it is an antique owned by a neighbor who let others use it after complaints were made about having something so big in the hallway!"

"I'm on your side. I'm just saying how they see things. There's also the matter of what happened in Chicago..."

"An accidental death."

"That's what I believe but..."

"A misogynous lunatic psychiatrist who kills women he can't control and sexually abuses those he can."

"Something like that."

"Can't beat it for copy. Jack The Ripper in New York. And believe it folks, he really was a doctor participating in your health plan."

Joan didn't say anything. I wondered if she believed I was innocent, or that anyone would.

The club was probably stained during one of my daily walks in Central Park. Before my energy became regularly exhausted by Gerri's kids, who I might never see again.

Joan cleared her throat.

"How many states did you live in before returning to New York?"

"Lots. Don't tell me."

"The police are checking the reports of women who disappeared in those states."

116

"Now I'm another Ted Bundy. What do *you* think?"

She didn't answer directly.

"Are you sure you want *me*? My cases are mostly white collar—CEOs cooking the books. Not murder, with publicity making you a lawyer's dream. Think about it. You don't have to decide now."

I did think. Too many things were happening too quickly and I needed stability to be able to plan. I didn't know how good a lawyer Joan was. The only personal things about her I knew was that she had attended a Chicago law school, was about my age, and was the single mother of a delightful seven year old.

One day Joan had decided that she wanted to have a child. There being no steady man in her life, she became pregnant by her temporary boyfriend.

But Joan refused to have his name on the birth certificate, stating that he was too unreliable to be a father. She insisted on this despite the judge's concern, stating that she would care for her daughter, and she always did.

Joan had three previous abortions. She gave birth this time, and eventually graduated from law school. It took her an extra year because she had to earn money by working part-time for a newspaper, covering local events and writing an advice-to-the lovelorn column.

One of her celebrated responses was to a woman who loved oral sex but refused to swallow the "awful tasting" semen. Joan related this to its acidity, described the taste as being similar to "watery tapioca pudding flavored with bleach," and suggested a change in the boyfriend's diet.

117

While *I* was mightily impressed with this response it, and being over forty, didn't help during her law school admission interviews where she was told that by the time she graduated she would be too old to join the Young Lawyers Association.

So despite her Law School Admission Test score being better than that of ninety nine of every hundred other applicants, she was accepted by only one—*third-rate*—law school. Graduation from which usually dooms a legal career since no other profession is as status conscious. So Joan wasn't likely to be socializing with the prosecutor's Ivy League trained staff.

I added up her advantages and disadvantages.

Most importantly, I needed someone *now* to start figuring out my crazy situation, and her reporter background meant that she would be good at ferreting information.

But she did have four drawbacks.

One. I knew, though illogical, that women weren't taken as seriously as men.

Two. She was inexperienced but this wasn't crucial since some professionals are just repeating their same mistakes for years.

Three. Her lack of intimacy with the prosecutor. A lawyer's ability to negotiate before entering the courtroom can be more important than what happens there, where anything might.

Four. Also—her life style. Jurors tend to be conservative. How would they react were they to learn of her three abortions, being a deliberate single parent, *and* the past writer of a lovelorn column (in which she had also discussed her personal life and beliefs)? Would they still take her seriously, or laugh me into the death house?

Yet I felt I had no choice. Whether her disadvantages outweighed her advantages I didn't know. But I knew that she cared about me and might even believe I could be innocent. Moreover, her personal life was so atypical that mine wouldn't trouble her.

I also sensed that she was a fighter and wouldn't give up until the end, which we both hoped wouldn't be mine. *No* client's death sentence advances their lawyer's career.

These thoughts raced through my mind as Joan watched. I knew that she wanted a cigarette and Irish Coffee, heavy on the whiskey, these being other of her politically incorrect vices. But she never drank, or smoked while she was pregnant or when she was at home—even before she learned that her daughter was asthmatic. Joan was a good mother, which was another reason that I favored her.

"Well?"

I swallowed and was grateful not to have an Adam's apple, which would now be visibly bobbing. Sensing my hesitancy about hiring her wouldn't improve her work.

"I want *you*. How much retainer for a start?"

"Five thousand. Who can handle the financial details?"

I said to send the bills to Gerri even as I wondered if I would ever see her again. My little basic trust was being rapidly diminished by current events.

"I want you to breathe deeply while I'm speaking," she said. "You look like your mind is racing. Don't say anything—just listen. I never promise clients anything. You can't in law anymore than in medicine. Some criminal statutes aren't clear, and once you get into a courtroom everything can change depending on the whims of a jury, which may have little to do with the facts."

"What bothers me..." I started to say, until Joan interrupted.

"I told you to listen."

"I'm sorry but I need to get some things off my chest."

"OK, but there's information you should know and we don't have much time."

"I feel like I'm going crazy. Circumstantial evidence is being weaved together with innocent facts to make me into a monster. They've taken the narrowest darkest views to railroad me. They're even ignoring the fact that I've *treated* people in their agencies."

I didn't add that my electric chair nightmare seemed to be coming true. It was enough for one of us to be terrified.

"OK," she responded. "What you're saying is correct but irrelevant. The legal and jail systems have their rules and we must battle within them. Go outside their rules and we lose. We can bend them till *I* nearly wind up in jail but we have to follow them. First I'll tell you my rules, then the legal ones.

"One. You talk to no one about the case or your past. If this drives you crazy, listen to their problems.

"Two. Tell the truth only to me. Lawyer-client confidentiality is absolute but you have none with Gerri. Tell her that you love her and talk to her about the kids or a movie but not the case. Is that clear?"

"I shouldn't talk about the case or my life."

"You're a quick study—which is why I always wanted a doctor for a client."

"They also pay well," I said, and immediately regretted my words. "I'm sorry. I'm very angry," I added quickly.

"You don't have to apologize—you've a right to be angry. A lawyer is like a psychiatrist and will never reject a client so long as their rules are being followed. But the rules aren't written in stone."

I had nothing to say. I was just thinking that I didn't make a mistake in hiring her.

"Now for my plans. I'll tell Gerri the basics, and try to get bail. As you said, you have an impeccable reputation and the evidence seems circumstantial. Follow my lead in court. There, even an apparently reasonable statement can haunt you later so don't say more than I tell you.

"Then I'll find out what's on the prosecutor's mind though we can't count on their having made stupid mistakes. After which we have to talk about who Louise was and may have been involved with. If doctors killed every patient they didn't like we solo lawyers wouldn't be in such bad financial shape.

121

"The election may be influencing matters. Upwardly striving lawyers love high profile cases though this D.A. was around so long and is so certain of reelection that I can't conceive of it influencing him. But he's old—maybe jockeying for his job has already begun.

"Now about the jail. You're lucky that the police are experimenting with new procedures. My last client was also from this precinct."

"My neighbor-in-crime," I blurted out.

"Your neighbor-in-crime," she agreed, without a smile, continuing her well-organized monologue. It didn't sound rehearsed but good speakers don't.

"Ordinarily by now you'd be going through processing at Central Booking. You're here because the City is trying to keep the police close to their precinct to avoid paying overtime. There have been lawsuits about conditions at Central Booking. Is Gerri home this morning?"

"She works from home doing market research. Call before you go—her kids hear everything."

"Of course. Is there anything else you want to tell me now?"

"No. So I'll see you in a few hours?"

"Yes, and try not to worry. I tell every client this though I don't know how much they can follow the advice. The justice system takes time and if you spend each day worrying you'll be worn out when important things happen. Trust me to tell you when you should worry.

"Thinking about your situation is OK but obsessing saps your energy. Remind yourself that you're a decent guy with bad luck. Like someone walking on a sidewalk who got hit by a car. No rational person would have expected it."

After these words and a handshake she left and I felt better, having been reminded again of how good support feels.

CHAPTER TWENTY TWO

FOR THE FIRST time since my military service I realized how slowly time goes when your life depends on others. Until the time for court I would be alone with Isaac. Sometime later we would get breakfast. Maybe I would be issued the orange jumpsuit I noted on prisoners in those days when I was only a psychiatrist. My change from independence to dependence came quickly yet seemed familiar, like having returned to childhood.

My father was also a physician, one of those unfortunately too common doctors who are unable to cope with their patients' feelings. In a rare personal comments to me he described an incident from when he was an intern.

My father was accompanying a cancer specialist who had to inform a husband of his thirty-one year old wife's impending death. The man cursed both of them and accused them of bungling. That night my father decided to specialize in pathology, the medical specialty which required the least contact with patients.

My mother was also an odd one, being the daughter of a black sheep son from an enormously wealthy family. Think Dupont or Mellon and you have some idea of how much money there was.

Her father settled his wife and children on four thousand acres in upstate New York, to shield them from the corrupting influence of civilization (as he viewed it).

My mother and her four sisters were educated privately at home. All rebelled as adults, one example of which might be what caused her conversion to my father's Judaism, not that he cared. And this was before it was chic (in some quarters) to be Jewish. Like most converts she became more observant than those born to the faith.

I haven't seen my aunts in years. One became a drug addict, the rest were alcoholic. I remember my grandmother as being a slight, kindly woman who brought rich cookies when she visited. A welcome treat for my parents, who were both doctors, were into healthy eating and would sooner give their son a spinal tap than a cookie. It never ceases to amaze me how crummy parents can become commendable grandparents. Probably its the emotional distance which makes this possible.

Now, lying on a bunk staring at the yellow colored wall, a hue which was likely chosen because it was believed to relax prisoners, I wondered for the umpteenth time why my life had remained solitary despite there being many girlfriends who would have welcomed marriage with me.

During my psychiatric residency I became involved in a dispute deriving from my tactless behavior with everyone but patients.

The assistant director of the department, Dr. X, was separated from his wife and living with a much younger nurse. We (the nurse and myself) began brief marriage counseling with a middle-aged couple—who she quickly reamed into.

"What happened to the love in your life? Why can't you say that you love each other?"

Likely they had *never* said it. And to insist that people who can't tolerate feelings suddenly express them causes major stress and possible psychological collapse. Her words horrified me.

So after they left *I* boomed at *her*.

"What did you think you were doing? We're seeing them for just a few sessions. Who'll put 'em back together then?"

You can guess what happened. She tearfully complained to her boyfriend who criticized my "abrasive personality" at a faculty meeting and insisted that I be thrown out of training. I considered this excessive but she was *really* seductive. Far different from his wife who I met at the medical school's Christmas party—along with their six kids.

Despite my anxiety, for to be dismissed from one's residency is a major medical career derailment, nothing happened and the decision (for those in the know) was predictable.

The department's director, a Mormon with nine children, didn't like Dr. X, whose impending divorce would be the first among the medical staff. Sooo...I was invited to Sunday dinner with his family—and the nurse was ordered to receive further training in counseling. Shortly thereafter she and her doctor/boyfriend moved. To Los Angeles, where else?

I was doing my usual worrying while the director was deciding but, thankfully, was not alone. A month before, a woman in a neighboring apartment invited me to bed to keep warm after our first (winter) date. Which we did and had a great time sexually. She was very passive and whatever I wanted to do was OK by her which was fine by me. Then we talked.

"How old were you when you first had sex?" I asked.

"Twelve."

"You southern girls start early," I responded, with surprise. I was a virgin till I was twenty one, a fact which I didn't advertise. More bravado.

"Yeah, he was my father."

We dated for two months but never lived together. I told myself it was because she was just a high school graduate while I was *a doctor*. She had been a Playboy bunny and showed me her photo wearing ear flaps and net stockings. I wondered if she were also a prostitute from something I sensed, though the thought more likely derived from my inaccurate fantasy about Club waitresses. Obviously I didn't ask, having *some* tact.

This woman didn't know basic health information. She even slept in her hard contact lenses, which I insisted that she stop. Maybe we should have gotten married for I felt comfortable being with her and my stress disappeared as we lay together. Then our relationship was over and she was gone too. Another casualty of my not-so-loved life.

Recent events—arrest, strip-search, becoming and being with prisoners—was forcing me to confront issues I had but glanced over before. Like what I really wanted in life but never achieved. I only hoped that it wasn't too late.

CHAPTER TWENTY THREE

I ENTERED A dreamless sleep which provided me no answers, and awoke to the noise from the other cells, crescendoed by that of Isaac flushing the toilet.

After breakfast (oatmeal, bread, juice, milk, coffee) we were handcuffed, shackled, and led to an elaborately decorated courtroom. On two walls hung pictures of past justices of the New York State Court of Appeals, including one who ended his career in prison and was now busy trying to rehabilitate his image through public service.

Prisoners occupied the first row. Others were filled with those who were too carefully dressed to be relatives and were likely reporters. Only my case held public interest and I sensed that my career was plummeting.

The judge explained the constitutional rights which offering a guilty plea waived. Which could have reflected his fairness, or the presence of reporters and his re-election worries and need for good publicity.

The proceedings were brief, with the charges being read and each prisoner responding.

The Goon had urinated in the street. His "medical" reason wilted under the judge's glance and his public defender lawyer's stare. "Guilty," he asserted, when his plea was again requested. A smile lit his face as he was sentenced to thirty days in jail: he was going home.

The Rainbow Coalition's charges were disorderly conduct and interference with governmental operations. Their lawyer wore pinstripes and a regimental tie—probably a bowler hat too were this permitted in court.

"Boisterous lads, unused to the enticements of New York," he explained, and then speculated whether experiencing joy was a crime. He, the judge and the government attorney smiled before all whispered at the bench, perhaps scheduling a golf date.

After each pleaded guilty to one charge, their five day jail sentences were suspended and would be voided if they remained out of trouble for three months. I hoped to be so lucky.

Joan was dressed in a black jacket, silk blouse, and ankle length skirt. Too chic for court but maybe just right for reporters. My hands were moist and my stomach was queasy.

The charge was murder and I pleaded "not guilty." Joan emphasized my "impeccable professional reputation" and long residence in the city after her application for my bail was opposed.

The government counsel stressed the brutality of the homicide and my being under suspicion for having committed numerous others, with the potential death penalty increasing the risk of my flight. Joan replied that these charges were just rumors and that all of the current evidence was circumstantial. I hoped.

The judge looked pained though maybe he was just tired. Bail was set at five hundred thousand dollars, my passport ordered surrendered, and my trial was scheduled in three months. Proceedings ended, and I was returned to my cell to await my next meeting with Joan. She didn't look happy.

"Is it that bad?"

Joan didn't answer me directly. Maybe she was more nervous than me. Maybe hiring her *was* a mistake.

"It just means that we have more work to do. The blood on your walking stick *is* human. They're testing the hairs—I don't know what they can find."

"The age, sex, and ethnic group of the victim from the DNA autorad. It's like a bar code. It'll clear me."

"Could be."

Neither of us seemed optimistic. The rapid descent from an office to a jail cell didn't foster mine.

"Tell me briefly about Louise," Joan said.

"I can talk for hours."

"Save that for when you're out of here."

"She's was young, in her early thirties. I treated her until four years ago. She loved me."

Joan stiffened.

"It wasn't like that—I never touched her. It was her fantasy of me that she loved. I was the only one who knew all of her secrets yet still would never ask her for sex. Also I was the one who was always available, until finally I wasn't.

"She lost her job and started acting too crazy, trying to make therapy her life which it can't be. She wouldn't enter a day hospital program so I ended her treatment with me. But she still considered me her doctor and sent me signed letters, 'Your Patient,' though she had many therapists after me. They tried to help her but couldn't for reasons it would take too long to explain now. She probably felt that I deserted her."

Joan thought for a moment and then changed the subject.

"How well can you account for your life? When we get an estimated time of death."

"Ask about any weekday or Saturday morning and I can tell you where I was. But their time won't be precise. If there aren't witnesses they'll have to rely on post-mortem changes: body temperature; rigidity—rigor mortis; skin discoloration—livor mortis; and chemical changes like a clouded cornea."

"You sound like an expert."

"I forgot most of the physical medicine which I learned, like most psychiatrists do. My father was a pathologist. He was also emotionally dead but that's a story we don't have time for now though it would make another of my winning headlines: KILLER PSYCHIATRIST'S FATHER CUT UP BODIES TOO. LIKE FATHER, LIKE SON?"

"Ignore them."

"Can the jurors?"

"Sometimes, but the stories won't be all bad. It's good that people learn you're a doctor who works with kids. They're well thought of. In the abstract when your's isn't being treated, then sometimes not. I'll ask potential jurors whether they read about the case. Be glad that you're not an insurance exec. People would pay to watch your execution...sorry."

"We both know where I stand. What are my odds?"

"It's too early to say. I don't yet know all the evidence, though odds don't count for much in court. I've lost and won cases without being sure why. Juries are unpredictable."

"So if I hope for a miracle one will happen?" I asked, thinking that my depression must be lifting if I was becoming my usual wise cracking self. But Joan took my silliness seriously.

"Always. Even homicide detectives do and they're more cynical than you. I dated one who was as hard as they come. 'It's easy to get like me,' he said, 'practice walking into a room and having a piece of brain fall on your head.'

He'd wake up seeing murder victims at the foot of the bed. We didn't date long. I understood why he joked like he did but I couldn't take it.

"He said that he was looking for a miracle. To arrest someone who seemed as guilty as they come but then discovering the truth and getting him freed. Maybe he was hungering for innocence in his corrupt world."

I had nothing to say, not even a bad joke.

"But some of his stories were funny. A guy was stopped for speeding and showed a stolen license. The cop looked at it and asked, incredulously, 'is your name Eileen?' He was told, 'sometimes I use that name.' A real New York story."

I laughed for the first time in twelve hours.

"OK, I'll expect justice."

"But getting it takes schmoozing DAs to see where things are. After you're released we'll talk more and get a sense of who Louise really was."

"I know who she really was."

"Maybe."

I let her criticism pass. You don't attack someone you're dependent on, this being a truism which it took me longer than most people to learn.

"How long will it be before I get out?"

"Just a few minutes with the court's new financial system. It was finally taken out of the dark ages."

She left, and I was sorry to see her go. Now I really understood why prisoners had so welcomed my professional interest: because I assured them that there still existed a world of courtesy. Where people had names not numbers, and eccentricities were respected. Like not wanting to be casually touched.

I never did liked being touched and only now learned how physical being a prisoner was. Touching was involved in taking fingerprints and being placed in handcuffs. Sometimes when being instructed what to do. I always believed that seemingly coincidental events often aren't. Like my choosing the only medical specialty where patients weren't handled.

Isaac was seated on his bunk when I returned. He was still unshaven and not looking any better than me. We were comrades sharing a foxhole, warring with the keepers of society.

"Did you talk to your parents about bail?" I asked. His was twenty five thousand dollars. He grinned and made the crack I thought of.

"Are you really worth twenty times me?"

"I'd change places. Like I said to a friend who was divorcing a crazy woman we both dated, 'Things could be worse. *I* might have married her.'"

"I'm getting out this morning. Can I do something for you?"

I was touched. He seemed to mean it—and from a guy I had met only hours before.

"Thanks, but I expect to be getting out too. Let's keep in touch. Maybe we can help each other."

We had no pen or paper but his hyphenated Russian-Spanish name was the only in the Brooklyn directory and I was the one Chinese sounding psychiatrist located on Central Park West. More illusions of this polyglot city.

CHAPTER TWENTY FOUR

Joan did her part, Fidelity Investments did theirs, and I was released before noon. Isaac had left a half-hour earlier and we shook hands warmly, now being brothers in America's largest fraternity.

Joan drove me to Gerri's apartment and reminded me, before she left, of our appointment later that day. I stood hesitantly by the building's door. Twenty-four hours before I had a psychiatric practice and deepening relationship. Now I wasn't sure that either existed or would for long.

The City was teeming but Beekman Place was quiet, a relief from the noise of the precinct house. I leaned against the building and watched passersby, feeling like the stranger in another of my childhood dreams where I wandered alone to the Bowery.

As I entered the building I wondered whether news of my arrest had already been published, so I went to the corner newsstand for the tabloids. I achieved page two in the *Daily News* and page three in the *Post*. Clutching these, I returned to greet the doorman who gave me the curt remark which he granted to all temporary roomers-in. Notorious or not, that was my status in this building.

I courteously held the elevator for one tenant and then another tenant. Waiting for a third would seem bizarre.

Minutes later, too soon I felt, I was turning the key in the lock as the door suddenly opened. Gerri stood looking at me.

While thinking downstairs, I had planned to say, "I didn't kill her." And I hoped that she would then respond, "I'd never believe it." But this didn't happen. When the door closed, I just started crying.

I cried only once before but had now experienced too much. With my arrest and the death in Chicago becoming public knowledge, I had no one to go to except Gerri. I wondered if she still wanted me. Would any sane woman?

Finally, with my emotions back under control, I knew that we had to talk.

"Your collar's wet," I said.

She smiled. It was pained, but still a smile.

"It'll dry." She squeezed me tighter. "How was it?"

"Not so bad. Maybe I'll write an article about another kind of managed care. Where are the kids?"

"Next door, camping out in sleeping bags. It's great fun for them though they insisted on having your pancakes for breakfast."

"Have you told them?"

"I didn't know what to say."

In the past I had advised others how to cope with a parent's arrest but had never expected to need this knowledge in my life.

"They're very young. Wait till they ask. Then give only one or two sentences."

We didn't talk much. I could deny killing Louise or any woman in the many places I lived but if I needed to say this then our relationship was already over.

"Let's go to bed," she said. Like those who want to make love after a funeral, affirming life when confronting oblivion. I kissed her forehead.

"OK, I'll shower first."

"Let's shower together."

"No, I want to be alone. I'll be right in."

I stayed under the hot water more than a few minutes, trying to dissolve the day's memories. Then I remembered that I had to meet Joan and finished washing quickly. I was a doctor with a waiting lover. With whom he didn't have sex for he wanted only to be held. Which Gerri did until it was time to leave.

"It won't be easy," I said. "I'm today's pop headline. If you stay with me, you'll get involved. Should I move back to my apartment."

"This *is* your apartment."

"You know what I mean."

Gerri looked down, and then directly at me.

"My life was never easy. Besides, no man who treats children as loving as you do can be a murderer. Soon the police will know this and we'll have only our normal problems again."

I hugged Gerri tightly and was grateful for her support though I knew that what she believed wasn't true. Ted Bundy, before his electrocution for just three of the many women he killed, was wonderful with kids.

I left her apartment, being unsure whether I would return. I longed to remain but knew what reporters could inflict on even involuntary participants in publicized events.

CHAPTER TWENTY FIVE

Joan practiced law out of two rooms which she sublet from another law firm's unused space. Which was common in these days of burgeoning numbers of law school graduates and decreasing fees. Neither of us looked happy and I didn't try making a joke. Not even a bad one like referring to her tasty semen response in the long ago newspaper column. Joan was now a Parent-Teacher Association president, budding lawyer, and my only hope.

"How is my defense going?"

"We don't have one yet. Just the government's friendly attitude which bothers me."

She looked away while speaking, as if she felt more comfortable telling me bad news when she wasn't facing me. Then she forced a small smile. "Which just means that we have more work to do."

"Like the doctor said, 'you have a small growth...'"

"It's not like that."

"How is it?"

"The odds continually change. I once won as hopeless a murder case as a lawyer ever gets though the verdict wasn't what most would call justice.

"I didn't know."

"No. So maybe hiring me wasn't as dumb a decision as you sometimes think."

After she spoke I felt closer to her, thinking, again, that despite her recent graduation from a third rate law school she was turning out to be more than OK.

"What happened?"

"I thought that you'd never ask," she said, now with a real smile. "Do you want coffee. I can get it from the lounge. Yogurt too." As we ate (Dannon Nonfat Vanilla for me, Blueberry for her), she began speaking.

"After law school I worked as a public defender. Being inexperienced, I couldn't get another job. I was also a new mother with *big* boobs. I knew the way some interviewers stared they wanted me but were afraid of being sued. And I'm not coming on to you though if you weren't involved with my best friend when we met I would have. You're attractive and good with kids. And I like your shy act but I never bought it."

As Joan spoke, I thought of the different ethics which doctors and lawyers have. While being attracted to occasional patients, I never spoke to them as she just did to me. Even after a newly divorced girl friend told me that, while lying naked on the examination table with the fingers of her smiling gynecologist probing, she was forced to ask that he hold his chatty questions until she was dressed.

And another woman wondered why, after presenting the identical symptoms to two doctors, one requested that she strip above the waist while the other wanted to investigate her below.

Joan paused. A cacophony of horns blew outside, the typical Manhattan backdrop for daily events and crises.

"I convinced a jury to free a drug selling murderer. I saved him from the electric chair."

The pulsing fear from my electrocution nightmare regurgitated as she continued her story.

"The judge was a bitch who wanted killers executed and decided their guilt *before* trial. It was in a southern state which was weighed down by centuries of paternalism. Prejudice too, but not racial. The defendant was black but the judge would have felt the same about a white one.

"It was a drug deal gone bad and my client shot the guy. There was no doubt about it. The police and forensics were competent. They even found the gun with his fingerprints on it. Perry Mason wouldn't have taken this case.

"The only thing I had to use was the defendant's age: he was just seventeen at the time of the murder. I dreaded having to visit him in the Death House and needed to emphasize his youth to save him. It was my only card.

"But every time I tried to raise this issue, the judge warned me. Finally she threatened me with contempt which with her meant going to jail. I had a young child and couldn't risk it. So the next to last day of the trial I took all the papers in front of me, tore each into little pieces, and tossed them into a wastebasket. Seven pages, one at a time. Taking long minutes while the jury watched.

"They slowly realized what was happening: that the judge wanted this boy/man dead and was keeping me from defending him.

"They no longer cared that I wasn't a churchgoer and he had been a drug dealer. They wanted a merciful justice and weren't about to let someone be executed for something he did at seventeen!"

Joan stopped. Another dramatic pause though her story didn't need it. I'd practically stopped breathing.

"What did you do?"

"It was what the judge did: she overreached herself. She gave the jury a choice of only two verdicts: 'guilty,' meaning his execution, or 'not guilty.' Deliberations took less than an hour and I drove the boy and his mother home."

The emotion from her story pounded through me as a question nagged. "How could you manage the case after destroying your notes?"

"*Notes*?" she responded with a small smile, "they were blank sheets of paper."

Her sober look brought me back down to earth. "Now, describe Louise to me. Then I'll tell you how the DA sees things," she said.

CHAPTER TWENTY SIX

WHAT I TOLD Joan about Louise wasn't all that much. Psychiatrists learn mostly what is on their patients' minds and Joan wanted to know how Louise spent her days and who she knew. So describing her took less time than one would expect, considering that I treated Louise for many years and received letters from her afterward.

I tried convincing Joan that if I was guilty of anything it was only of trying to heal someone who was incurable. I knew that if she believed this she would do her best to save me but I wondered if she did.

"Louise never had much money and I never charged her much so maybe the saying that no good deed goes unpunished is true. After losing her job she began behaving really crazy, and too much trouble. So when she was hospitalized the next time, I asked her doctor not to send her back to me for her psychotherapy. Louise called me when she got out and I said that if she stayed in a program for three months I would treat her but I knew that she couldn't. Now I feel really guilty. Maybe if I had kept treating Louise she would still be alive—and I wouldn't be here."

Joan crossed her legs, which gave me a view of her panties. Many divorcing female patients told me that their lawyer had tried to seduce them. Maybe Joan was turned on by a man needing help, or was looking for a father for her daughter. Or she was just doing what men do. Using all of their assets to keep a well-paying client from taking his legal business elsewhere.

"I want to give you some advice, then I'll tell you the state's motive," she said. "Don't mention *guilt* again. Jurors look for black/white answers and this word will stick in their minds. You must think of yourself only as a healer. The image you present must be that of the kindly doctor who sought and seeks only healing for his patients.

"You could predict the state's logic. A man has brief involvements with many women which suggests that he has serious emotional problems with them. After murdering his first victim—which is misinterpreted as an accident—he kills again in different locations until his desire is satisfied.

"Then he returns to New York City where he lived during his childhood. Eleven years later he starts killing again. The absence of rape is evidence that his motive wasn't sexual.

"Maybe it was rage toward women: Louise's face was battered before her body was burned. Her hands and feet were removed with surgical skill—to dehumanize her.

"She could be identified only through a letter which was found in a corner. Something which was written while she awaited her murderer. The tiny clue which detectives believe that every killer overlooks."

"See the autopsy case file," I said, hoarsely. "It's a professional opinion in a twelve by fourteen envelope. Maybe she was using drugs now." Then, calmer, I added, "I can pick holes in their argument."

"So can I but their evidence is good. It includes practice copies of sex letters which she sent you."

"I never got any. She never had sex with me or anyone. She was terrified of feelings and would never let a man touch her. That could happen only if she was raped."

"Forget that word. You must seem non-sexual, harmless."

"Yes ma'am."

Her eyes cringed and I regretted my comment.

"I'm sorry."

"It's not necessary."

She re-crossed her legs but now I averted my eyes from her definitely purple panties. This peeping resulted from my feeling terrified, which was causing me to regress.

"Let's go over the other evidence. The draft of a letter saying that she was meeting you at the time they believe she was murdered. A bloodstained club with her hair fibers, and your fingerprints on the handle. These match those on your pistol permit application."

"Another argument against gun registration laws," I said, being unable to restrain myself.

"What?"

"A silly joke. I'll shut up."

Joan shook her head slightly, perhaps wondering what caused her to find me attractive. Then she itemized more of the evidential threads which were strangling me.

146

"The club also has varnish dust which matches that from the warehouse, and fibers from your sweater were found in her room. Giving them another great motive: that you feared the loss of your medical license if her sex charges became public. Which is a much better reason for killing than the man who shoots his wife after she files for divorce and happens every day."

I must have looked gloomy because Joan touched my knee.

"Their best proof won't look so good after my experts attack it. But prosecutors aren't dumb: they can be impulsive and wrong, even criminal, but are never stupid.

"We have to understand Louise and no one knew her better than you so you have a lot of thinking to do. Tell me more about her."

I thought about the last time I saw her in the street.

"She changed over the years. In some ways but not others. She became more self-assured and took better care of herself. She was still fragile but sturdier than you'd expect. And she probably knew more people than both of us: her address book was filled."

"I'll ask if the police found it. Go on."

"I'm telling you my memories as they occur. *Free association*, psychoanalysts call it."

"That's fine."

Joan wrote as I spoke. I made a mental note to review Louise's record but didn't doubt what I was saying. I would never forget her.

"She enjoyed being beaten—maybe this had a sexual element."

"How do you know?"

"Because I used to beat her." Then, noting her changed expression, I quickly added, "I'm just joking. I better not kid like this. It's enough that one of us is terrified."

"I don't scare easily," she said, though looking wary. As if my statement had triggered something: the thought I was guilty, or crazy. Or maybe *she* enjoyed beating people. I imagined another headline: MONSTER PSYCHIATRIST'S LAWYER IS *THE* "MADAM PAIN." My reverie ended and I resumed speaking.

"She once went to a man's apartment. I don't remember where she met him...rambling again."

"Keep going."

"There were bolts in the wall he wanted to tie her to before beating her. She wouldn't go along with this but did let him spank her. Her father used to spank her, which I considered sexual. But she never had sex though maybe she kissed a man. It's so long ago that I'm not sure."

"You're doing well. Her tendency to please sadistic men indicates other murderer possibilities. Is there anything else?"

I thought. First deliberately, then letting my mind wander. Moments passed. I was aware of traffic sounds but nothing else. Then something did arise, with the suddenness of everything which spurts from the unconscious.

"She loved me but not sexually. There never was sex in her letters to me. Just her insistence that I was her best doctor and wanting me to treat her again. Or maybe sex *was* there and I was afraid to see it: my power over her was too great."

"That's too deep for me. Lawyers are down-to-earth like the police. I'd forget what you just said. It sounds like more evidence for the D.A.'s motive."

"Right!"

My morbid humor told me that being a live cheerleader was better than a dead doctor. The even better alternative seemed flight.

During my psychiatric training I worked evenings, evaluating the suitability of ex-convicts for jobs. But what I actually did went far beyond my expected duties. I created phony work histories for them, then had them practice details of their new/old lives. This worked and their hiring rate skyrocketed.

The head of the training program took his bows followed by the mayor and labor commissioner. Only once was I was identified: a manager suggested that I wear a tie so the office looked more professional. He backed off after learning that I was a doctor. Nobody messed with us then.

I was surprised at how easy forging these life stories was. My most difficult prospect had served twenty seven years for so vicious a crime that even I, then a budding psychiatrist, gagged when reading of it. But by forty nine he had been so cowered into submission by the prison system that he would never again be dangerous. Contrary to popular fear, paroled murderers rarely kill again. Except for serial killers of course.

I falsified his past and then sent him out. A year later I received the "thank you" letter from him which had been suggested by his bride who was pleased with their ownership of a new two-family house, car, and furniture. I felt proud, more so since the letter was written on his job's (a bank) stationery.

Louise loved this story and her eyes beamed as I constructed *her* history. I related her unemployment to marriage, and her current job search to her husband's accidental death. I even thought of creating a dead child to increase sympathy for her but wasn't sure that she could carry off the role of a doubly bereaved widow.

Like Professor Higgins I was getting carried away. I even thought of giving her *two* marriages with just the first ending in divorce. The more I brainstormed the happier she looked though we finally stayed with one marriage. After a few rehearsals I sent her out on stage.

But my efforts failed since Louise was then unable to work. And despite my opposition she did adopt the role of a doubly saddened widow, this resulting in the offer of four jobs and many more dates. So my skill as a forger of identities remained good though I hoped that I wouldn't have to be the acid test.

"One more thing," Joan said. "We're dealing with evidence *and* politics. People in the other states want their serial murders to be solved so the fear can end. D.A.'s aren't concerned about niceties of evidence—the pressure on them is too great. Their voters are scared."

I was too. I knew that crime which people feared most, murder, occurred least often, and that serial killing was unique in its ability to arouse terror. The threat from a single homicide is over as soon as the murderer is caught since the risk doesn't extend beyond the victim. But with serial killings the body count grows and the police are considered increasingly incompetent as the public awaits the next news: the murder of someone like them. A victim selected by chance and dying only because of the unknown motives of a merciless stranger.

So even if the murders cease for years the lack of closure maintains anxiety while awaiting discovery of the next body, there not yet being demarcation which allows time for the fear to end and healing to begin.

We stood within each others psychological space. Kissing Joan would be easy if the circumstances were different. But my life was complicated enough with my having to juggle one girlfriend, a murder charge in this and soon other states, and a geometrically increasing number of reporters digging into my life. Adding overnights with Joan and relating as father to her daughter too required greater deceptive skills than even this psychiatrist could muster.

Joan said that she would call me when she had more information and I hung on her every word. Just like my patients did from me—those I still had left.

CHAPTER TWENTY SEVEN

THERE WERE NO reporters outside of my office but I tensely awaited my first confrontation with them. The day doorman just nodded to me but he had never spoken much. Tenants who I met were too courteous—or frightened—to refer to what they knew, though our greetings did seem briefer than usual. My arrest must have been on the news. Louise's murder was worth only brief mention: the death of another "street" person. My involvement gave the story "legs."

My office seemed the same—until I looked at the fax machine. A single line was written in the middle of the page: "You murdered in Chicago and I pray that you'll get what you deserve this time." Obviously one person didn't like me, they even going to the trouble of getting my fax number from a physician directory.

I wondered where to begin: to phone patients and confirm their appointments though the call's intention was to inform them that I was still in practice; or to wait and see what happened. Then I remembered a chat with a sergeant during my military training. I was puzzled why he shared information so far from my medical duties but he must have sensed a similarity between us.

"When entering a guarded perimeter, you must move slowly despite your fear. The more frightened you are, the slower you must move until you're sure of the enemy. Then you must become merciless—a killing machine."

I protested. I was a doctor and it wouldn't be moral. We sipped our drinks. He was retiring, a veteran of Korea and Vietnam. A survivor wanting me to survive.

"Nothing is more moral," he said. "You're different from the other doctors. They play at being soldier but you sense how to be one and am absorbing the craft.

"There's no higher morality than the soldier's creed: to be courageous with your unit, keep them alive, and to kill whoever tries to keep you from getting home.

"When you're not sure what to do, wait and look and listen. Then act like your country and family knows that you must."

So despite my anxiety, I waited. For a phone call or knock on the door—for anything. Then I dozed off, feeling too sad and tired to think anymore. I was awakened by the sound of the ringing telephone. My first observation was that my electrocution dream still had not returned. Then, that if one's daily life is a nightmare, perhaps it's unnecessary for the mind to create more.

It was The General.

"I'm calling to confirm tonight's appointment. I heard the news."

"I'll be here."

He hung up quickly, having stated only his first name, possibly fearing that the phone was tapped or knowing that it was. The General had a wide range of acquaintances, and colleagues gossip.

I calmed down and remembered other of the sergeant's advice: battles are won through training and planning, not impulsive movie type heroics.

Then I remembered what the ex-con said when I asked how he managed to survive twenty seven years in prison: "There's no difficulty a person can't overcome if he relies on himself."

I had relied on myself, but was I always alone? Often it seemed that confidential words were spoken and what I most feared—expulsion from training, legal or military consequences—never happened. But these were before my wanderings across America, and murder indictment.

Don't worry until you're facing a real concern and live one day at a time, Joan had advised.

The phone rang again.

"Dr. Yungg."

I repeated my name into the silence. Just before I concluded that it was a wrong number, an older man spoke with a heavy accent.

"Dr. Yungg, this is Enrico."

I thought quickly. He never came to his child's sessions; if more treatment was needed his wife would likely call. So, being ignorant of his intent, I adopted a chatty tone.

"How is your daughter?"

"Very good. She calls you 'my best friend' and talks about 'Benjamin'."

"A stuffed bear. I'm glad that she's well."

I waited, he waited, and I gave up first.

"How can I help you?" I asked, adopting the police lieutenant's words.

"I heard your bad news."

"Yes."

"You helped my daughter. My nephew's a lawyer and good at dealing with prosecutors."

I expected he was but associating my case with an attorney with even remote mob connections would condemn me with jurors.

"I'm grateful," I said, and meant it. "I have confidence in mine. If she doesn't work out I may well call him." Then, wanting to change the subject, I asked, "How is your daughter sleeping?"

"Now, she sleeps mostly through the night. When she comes into our room I say what you told my wife: that dreams are our friends and tell us what's going on inside of us, and she goes back to her bed."

"You're handling it well." Once again I was The Doctor In Charge. More silence.

"Legal matters can be like nightmares," he said. "Please call me if you need help. My wife prays for you. She bakes at Easter and will send you cookies."

I assured him I would call if I needed help, said I was looking forward to the cookies, thanked him and his wife, and our conversation ended.

We weren't as different as he might believe. My mother had difficulty breast feeding so I was fed her Italian friend's overabundance. And we both knew about nightmares.

CHAPTER TWENTY EIGHT

I WAITED AND, surprisingly, my patients did begin arriving. But only those I had treated for at least several months who apparently felt that, despite the frightening headlines, they knew the kind of person I was. Or maybe they shrank from having to reveal intimate matters to a new psychiatrist. Or because a murder accusation no longer had the same cachet now that business executives and politicians were being regularly indicted, even if not for homicide.

So I worked hard on my first day out of jail. And soon enough The General arrived, dressed in one of his hallmark gray double-breasted Dunhill suits and newer Turnbull & Asser shirts. He informed me of their manufacturers while regretting the closing of the Fifty Seventh Street Dunhill store, this adding to his unwelcome sense of aging.

He looked better than at his last session. Maybe he felt that his problems weren't bad compared with those of his doctor. Or maybe it was that psychotherapy does work and life goes on, no matter what is printed about me.

"How are things going?"

"That sounds like something I should be asking," he responded.

"I won't argue with that," I said, and gave my now by rote explanation. "I have a legal problem, a mistake which I expect will be worked out before long. I can't discuss it but like they say, 'don't believe everything that you read.'"

"I never do but am glad that you're optimistic. I would hate to have to find another therapist. One is enough for a lifetime."

"So, how are things going?" I repeated.

"Better than in your life."

Harold was being more cutting than usual.

"To dispute that I have to know what's happening."

The silence which followed was mostly because Harold found speaking of personal matters difficult. Maybe also because ordinary events can seem trivial when one's most recent job was advising the president.

"Did you have any dreams?" Another of my usual questions at the beginning of a session.

"Last night, but I don't remember much. I was sitting on a bench before a wide lawn. No one else was around and it seemed peaceful." Then he added, "Like in Bernard Baruch's photo—he was a financier and presidential advisor before your time."

"I'm not that uneducated."

Baruch died years before, having given advice which was reportedly more publicized than influential and losing more money in nineteen twenty nine's great depression than he would admit. But I sensed that Harold's *too deliberate* afterthought was unconsciously motivated and intended to conceal not inform. So *I* free-associated and my thought led to his earlier statement about Vincent Foster—who killed himself in a park.

158

"What else do you think it might mean?" I asked.

"Nothing. Just a dream."

"Dreams tell how a person views their life. During sleep when their psychological defenses are down and using symbols. These are like the clues in a mystery movie which must be put together for it to be solved. My association is your past comment about Vincent Foster killing himself in a park. Maybe you're telling yourself that you feel depressed." I spoke tentatively since hearing statements about one's unknown feelings can be upsetting.

"What does *depressed* mean?"

I was glad that Harold asked for, like most doctors, I enjoy acting the expert. So I gave that spiel.

"When a person feels depressed it's because they sense the depth of their problems, or are unsure what to do. So they give up and *depress* their feelings."

I risked saying more.

"We all make choices. What would you want to have achieved if you could live your life over?"

"Have a wife and at least one child. Some decisions I regret making. It's too easy to become involved by being accommodating, which is every military officer's style. You hear something illegal or distasteful, don't object, and suddenly find yourself having become part of a plan."

All psychiatrists are curious about their noted patient's lives and, more often than they should, live vicariously through them. But I didn't want to learn more.

Years before, when evaluating government workers, I heard stories about bosses who, fresh from their career of managing paperwork, would order subordinates into poorly planned, dangerous operations.

I preferred safe secrets: who was sleeping with who or using drugs. Even that of the teenager who graciously allowed his sister to invest her allowance in their school's drug selling network. But government secrets were of a different magnitude and I already had too many prosecutors arrayed against me.

Maybe Harold sensed this, or had reached his limit of self-disclosure. So, after shifting position and looking about the room, *he counseled me.* Possibly from not wanting to have to change doctor. But I think he was also grateful for my help, even if he was unable to admit this to either of us.

"Let me give you some advice. I've been a lawyer longer than I like to admit and read a lot more now that I'm retired. I know what to believe and sometimes what's really being said. But I don't understand why so many states are after you with only the one state's evidence that's been reported.

"I've dealt with killers. You're angry and controlled. Grandiose like many doctors, but not a killer. Though officials believe this and it's not easy changing their minds.

"You have to ask yourself: Why is all this happening to me? Whose apple cart am I upsetting? After figuring it out you can fight back. What's odd is that because you have money you can, and prosecutors don't like looking foolish so they may have more evidence than they're revealing.

"Let me tell you about lawyers and judges. More rambling from an old man who misses being listened to and now has to pay for it."

"If that's all I did you'd be wasting your money."

"I never do but I can see that you don't like being given advice. Interpret what I say if you must, but remember it!"

"People lie," he continued. "If presidents lie, as we now know all do, it shouldn't be surprising to learn that police and prosecutors will lie whenever they feel that it's in their interest to do so. Not all will lie, but expect it and you won't often be disappointed.

"Some lawyers see themselves as prophets or parish priests, others are thieves. One looted an estate he was executor for by inventing a phony heiress and registering in a motel dressed like a woman.

"Then there's the judge who prodded a lawyer with a dildoe—it wasn't reported where. Under the court trappings of grandeur there's humanity and stupidity though it's easy for a layman to be overawed.

"You'll feel shaky in court because you're being forced to confront the self-doubt and flaws which everyone has, suddenly and in public. Don't look for justice. *Sometimes* it happens, like the real truth coming out.

"An influential friend can be more valuable than the best lawyer. Ideally one has both."

There was little Harold said that I didn't know or Joan didn't tell me. But after my stay in jail I welcomed every indication of my value to another person.

My workday was over. I went home to Gerri, her kids—and my reporters. Not wanting to meet them at my building's entrance, I exited through the back door via a jungle of basement tunnels, like in horror movies which my life increasingly resembled.

While walking from Lexington Avenue towards First Avenue, I forced myself to breathe deeply and to walk slowly. Beside the entrance to Gerri's building, people talked in small groups. One woman caught my eye, then all of the reporters surged towards me, their pot of gold.

But they had their role and I mine. So I acknowledged I was Dr. Yungg, adding that I was advised by my lawyer not to speak with them. In almost less time than it takes to describe, I was within the waiting elevator (making a mental note to give the doorman a good tip for this service) and worrying about home.

There, life was as twenty four hours before. Gerri and the kids had already eaten and she was bathing them. Soon they kissed me goodnight. Then, when I was alone with Gerri, I didn't know what to say. Should I further describe my experiences or just insist that I needed her?

She spoke first.

"How was your day?"

"Better than I expected, even with the reporters. Did Joan phone?"

"Just. She left her home number."

Despite my anxiety about why she called, I felt too exhausted to move. Only now was I beginning to feel calm, being soothed by the ordinary sounds of children quarreling.

"How was your day?"

"My work or your reporters?"

"I didn't expect this either."

"I shouldn't have said that. It wasn't bad. Just that I wanted a more peaceful life than with Siggie. You're different, but..."

I felt angry at her criticism though less so than with past girlfriends. I seemed to be changing.

She forced my head onto her breast and I vented my feelings about the stupidity of the legal system, the sadism of the police, and my worries. Now, for the first time, I experienced that closeness which I never did as a child when I had told myself that I didn't need warmth. Like all children do when it's unavailable, lest their pain be too great.

While Gerri got my dinner I called Joan and heard her daughter in the background. Being told "Lew" was on the phone and to get into the bath, which she apparently did. Again I thought of how well-behaved a child living with a single parent becomes when a potential mother or father enters the scene.

"How did your day go?" Joan asked. Just like Gerri.

"Better than I expected with the patients. I avoided reporters by sneaking out the back exit of my building."

"It won't work again. They probably already know about it."

"Something new?" I asked, not wanting her to become too supportive. *One* girl friend and my problems were enough for now.

"Bad, and worse."

"Worst first." I said, always expecting this.

"The feds froze your assets under RICO though I don't see how it applies to you. You'll get the money back after you're cleared but without interest. It's too expensive to fight them."

Hopefully, they hadn't discovered the several brokerage accounts which I set up years ago under false social security numbers: evidence of my lifelong paranoia.

"What's the better news?"

"It comes in little pieces. A judge authorized a search of your office/apartment, *excluding* all records but Louise's."

"There's nothing in it which I'd object to anyone seeing. Is a certified copy OK?"

"Always. But bring the original record to court. *If* the case gets that far."

"You're sounding pretty upbeat for someone who just learned she might not get paid."

"To feed me and my daughter," she said with a brief laugh, then became serious.

"It's still circumstantial. The autopsy file came and we'll go over it."

Our conversation ended with her (repeated) advice that I shouldn't worry until she told that I had something to worry about.

Gerri was still in the kitchen when I returned to the living room. Having joined my commitment to a low-fat diet, she no longer ate meat or eggs and I ate small pieces of goat cheese, her favorite. I would have the lowest cholesterol level on Death Row if I appeared for trial.

Dinner was fish and salad and whole wheat bread and wine and no more talk. Then bed, where she again held me until I fell asleep. But my nightmare this night wasn't of the familiar electric chair. At those times I woke silently. Now Gerri shook me, being afraid that the kids would hear my screams.

In the dream I was walking down First Avenue looking for a tall, elderly stranger who planned something which I had to stop, even by killing him. I was afraid that I wouldn't find him in time. I looked at my watch and realized that I had missed the appointment, and then remembered that he was waiting on the more elegant Park Avenue and that someone had told me something important but not who or what. A policeman noticed my distress and asked if he could help. I became enraged and was beating him with my fists when Gerri woke me.

"The same dream?" Only she and my dead analyst knew of it.

"No, a new one."

I didn't want her knowing that in the dream I was trying to kill someone for being helpful. She was already nervous enough about me.

"I couldn't find someone and panicked."

"You were yelling."

"Could you make out what I said?"

"You were just repeating 'no, no.' You hit me."

"I'm sorry—it's everything I'm going through. I'm a peaceable guy though no one wants to believe it."

"If I didn't think that would I trust you with my children?"

When I next woke it was caused by their voices and still early enough for me to make them breakfast. This task always calmed me, even when they demanded what wasn't available. But that morning went easy: either they sensed my distress or it was one of their good days. Now it was blueberry pancakes, spilled milk, and silliness. Later, decaffeinated coffee and more talk with Gerri.

I hated having to tell her of my precarious financial situation, knowing how important financial stability is to a mother. Unexpectedly, she wasn't bothered. "Kirsten has a trust fund I can draw on for essentials."

"Who set it up?"

"Her godfather after she was born."

"He should have opened one for Karen too."

"He could afford it. He has only sons and maybe when Kirsten was born he felt the need for a daughter."

"I'm glad—I was worried. I always considered it a man's responsibility to support his family. Maybe that's why I never married: because I was afraid that I would fall down on the job, and now I did."

"You couldn't have known."

"Not about Louise. My treatment was the best which I could give her but I still feel guilty."

"You always do. Even when the pancakes burn you criticize yourself. It's in a silly way and the kids like it but you're really angry though they don't see that. They just think that you're being 'silly Lew' again and boss you around."

"That helps kids feel comfortable."

"With them you don't change the subject by 'acting doctor.'"

"Another of my personality faults," I agreed.

"We all have them," she said, an observation which I had often made to others.

"Yes...have they mentioned my arrest yet?"

"Nothing."

"It's beyond their day-to-day world unless someone taunts them. Or their day care expels them."

"So I'll find another."

"Boyfriend or day care?" I asked, adding another to my lifetime collection of the dumb comments I made to women. But she didn't criticize this for she knew how difficult it was for me to trust.

"You don't need any promises from me. I'm yours, and we'll get out of this mess."

CHAPTER TWENTY NINE

Fᴇᴀʀɪɴɢ ᴛʜᴀᴛ ʀᴇᴘᴏʀᴛᴇʀs would follow me even onto a bus, I now took a taxi to my office. Where the doorman nodded as he usually did, though adding a mocking—or supportive?—smile. To which I gave my own slight smile, before riding the empty elevator to meet with the Reverend Cary McMasterby, who sat by my door.

In the office he accepted coffee like The General did. Both were definitely feeling more comfortable with therapy. As was our silence.

"Two sinners over their morning coffee."

"What do you mean?" I wanted to know where he was "at."

"I read about you in the papers. I didn't sense that you were single."

I waited for him to say more.

"Will you be keeping your practice open?"

To this now familiar question, I gave my practiced spiel, then added, "How do you feel about the arrest?"

"I'm here because of *my* life." His words supported my long-held conviction that a doctor should not reveal their personal details to patients.

"How are things going?"

"Like they were with Kierkegaard."

"The nineteenth century philosopher?"

"He was much more than just that."

"So educate me."

"He was physically grotesque having one leg shorter than the other. Though he still managed to win the love of his life, but then rejected her. He was always dissatisfied. He studied theology but was never ordained, and called a church official 'that liar of blessed memory.' He had a way with words."

"Like you do," I said, and wondered why I had interrupted him for this was poor therapeutic technique.

"Yes. Didn't they teach you never to interrupt?" Cary was justifiably angry so what he was saying must be important.

"Kierkegaard was moody. He'd be 'up' in public but depressed and guilt-ridden when he was alone. He was even upset about not being 'roasted' in the magazine, *Corsair*, because he knew the editor. Meir Goldschmidt. He was probably a Jew like you.

"One day he asked to no longer be spared criticism. Then his misshapen body was mocked so well that kids taunted him and parents scolded, 'Don't be a Sören!'

"Maybe he wanted to be a martyr or was sick with what they call a chemical imbalance today. But what he wrote did strike a chord: that only after a person is profoundly unhappy can their life become meaningful."

"What attracts you to his philosophy?"

"His backdrop on life. It frees you from daily 'noise' and gives perspective."

169

"Like religion."

"Yes. For Kierkegaard's philosophy *is* religious. His basic idea is that profound change can only occur after a person had a radical experience. Both Christians and Jews believe that people are ready for a 'return' and the coming of the Messiah. Which can happen *only* after they achieve full humanity through righteousness, or lose it through sin."

Cary sipped his coffee.

I wondered how he correlated his theology with being a sexual abuser but felt that asking this directly would upset him. So I investigated indirectly.

"How do you combine your religious beliefs with your life?"

"*Are* you Jewish, like every New York psychiatrist."

"My father was Jewish. My mother was Episcopalian originally."

Cary smiled. Not a frequent event in his therapy.

"A fellow Christian."

"Not really. My mother converted to Judaism before marriage and later became more religious than most of the synagogue members."

I wondered why I told him this for he was now my only patient who ever knew. Then again he was the only patient who had ever asked my religion.

Cary ignored my facts.

"A fellow Christian." This time his tone was openly mocking. Apparently, like the other clergy I treated, he felt more comfortable considering me Jewish, an outsider.

"Getting back to your life, which is what I'm being paid for. How do you reconcile your faith with it? As a psychiatrist I dress more formally than most. How are *you* affected by your profession?"

Cary was silent for several moments. Then, after gazing at the sky, he again faced me.

"I never completely fit into a religious vocation," he said. "Philosophically I did, but not personally."

"What would you want to be if not a clergyman?"

"A therapist in prison."

"Why?" I couldn't imagine a drearier work setting.

"I was a chaplain intern at Manhattan Correctional and got to know the prisoners."

"Any in particular?"

"A man was awaiting sentencing for killing his wife after learning of her affair. He was filled with remorse. He said he had changed and now believed that only sinners who recognize how evil people can be would be among those He came to save. That others resent God's impossible demands, they just want for Him to live and let live. That he had come to understood why Christ came, and prayed to be healed. I was very moved."

Now I wondered if Cary's sexual abuse derived from his unconscious need for punishment? He seemed to feel very guilty about something. No wonder he remained with a doctor who he might sense was equally as guilt-ridden: an accused serial killer, and betrayer of innumerable women.

It was another good session. How ironic, I thought, that my professional work improved even as my life crumbled. Maybe *I* would have been more content in a religious vocation, where tradition weighed over the continuous self-exploration required for a psychiatrist.

But if so, which religion? My parents were Jews though some would not consider my mother's religious conversion as being valid since it was not performed according to Orthodox ritual. And, because in Judaism a child's religion is passed down by their mother, they would view me as being gentile.

So perhaps, being neither fully Jewish or Christian, I had long felt alienated, though I sensed that religion played but the smallest part. Maybe it was my being an only child with two working parents, reared by nannies and apparently being valued just for his academic achievements.

I began speaking later than most children. *After* I was brought to a child psychologist, to whom I revealed adult-like perceptions. Like when my grandfather carried me down from the dock to his boat I ordered him to "be careful." Which my mother, who knew him best, considered an appropriate demand indeed.

My parents were impressed with my intelligence— the psychologist was more concerned with my destructiveness and bullying. Though all are now dead, I'm still basically the same.

So it is likely that, after entering a profession where I was expected to be solicitous, my rage became sublimated into a fascination with guns: I was the only doctor in my army class who *loved* weapons training. I even took an elective course in explosives which, likely, made me the only member of the American Medical Association who is fully qualified to demolish a bridge.

No, I never fit into any religion. Or into my extended family with a "monster" grandfather and certified crazy aunts.

As my thinking ended, Cary showed his feeling that the session was over by shifting his position. Which, both psychologically and in clock time, it was.

The rest of the day was untroubled. I even got a new patient: a mother who wanted her daughter to be evaluated. Which caused my devious mind to fantasize that she was a reporter seeking a new angle on the nation's number one serial killer suspect ("DOCTOR YUNGG WAS ALONE WITH MY DAUGHTER" SAYS TERRIFIED MOTHER, the headline might read).

I dismissed this idea, believing that even newspaper ethics wouldn't permit involving a child in such activity. But maybe the girl was a young looking reporter, I then thought. Even President Nixon, arch-mistruster of the press, would have chuckled.

As I relaxed with such silliness, feeling relief at my work day being nearly over and anticipating comfort with Gerry and her kids, the phone rang. It was The General. He demanded to see me—"*now!*"

CHAPTER THIRTY

WHEN A PATIENT needs me *now,* either something is greatly upsetting them or they are angry and interrupting my schedule to cause me grief. Both are common events in the business of psychotherapy.

So I waited for Harold though I felt desperate to get home. In three months I might be on Death Row but now I was still a physician. Who was curious: why did *he* panic? Maybe I had been too impressed. An ex-presidential advisor isn't usual in any psychiatrist's practice. Not in New York or especially in Washington where "going for therapy is the kiss of death," as one politician put it.

Harold's tie was askew, his collar opened, and he refused my offer of coffee. I put my feet on the hassock and waited, knowing that he would speak eventually.

"Tell me again how confidential what I say is."

"What you say stays between us. No one sees my notes and since you pay cash, no insurance forms are filed. I resist subpoena—and most aren't valid for medical records."

More silence.

"Did you ever hear of the SOF?"

"Special Operations Forces?"

"Even psychiatrists aren't *completely* ignorant."

First sarcasm from Cary, and now from Harold. But I knew that if a patient felt comfortable enough when with to mock me, then I must be doing at least something right.

"I don't know much about them," I added, and Harold began his lecture, which seemed well practiced.

"SOF are small teams of soldiers who operate behind enemy lines in wartime. They tend to be distrusted and misused, because their commanders aren't trained in their capabilities. They sprang from the U.S./Canadian 1st Special Service Force of World War Two.

"These soldiers were eccentric and greatly feared. Particularly after they put stickers with their insignia on the foreheads above the German throats they slit. They were brave: eighty percent were killed or wounded. Not like being at the Pentagon where getting promoted depends on being agreeable, which I wasn't always. Most officers worry about their pension but I had family money—and files: paper copies at home with copies on CDs elsewhere. There are thefts even on secure army bases.

"What's in these files is what you might expect. Crimes which were never prosecuted, fraud cases which were settled too rapidly, sex—you'd be surprised at how juvenile an officer can behave. But I accommodated for I knew that real change comes only with political pressure. So I helped people whenever I could and never asked for any favors."

Harold paused. "I'll take that coffee now."

I was tired but I made it. Like Harold said, it's easier to go along. If I objected I might advance a notch up his annoyance list and angry patients cause trouble.

It didn't take me long. When I returned he seemed calmer, as if he had made a decision.

After several sips, with the cup on the low file cabinet beside him, Harold resumed speaking.

"It started after I became liaison between the SOF and other branches. For oversight, not operations, like helping to resolve disputes over weapons allocation. I was considered a 'good communicator' and knew others on the committee.

"SOF's representative kept boiling over. To smooth things, I was asked to 'get personal.' Which wasn't hard for we were similar: both never married, or quite fitting in. For years he had played chess against a computer, which I guess he had to: not many officers play chess. He also had a cat, which isn't favored in the military *or* politics. Dogs are *in*, cats are considered elitist.

"And he didn't look like a soldier, being short and thin. So this guy who we'll call 'The Colonel' had three strikes against him: he played chess, kept a cat, and didn't match Hollywood's image of a perfect soldier. But even so he was a good representative for the SOF because people didn't take him seriously. He didn't look like a warrior but he was deadly indeed.

"So we drank and played chess and watched videos of the old movies he loved: *Purple Noon* and *Alphaville*. Never Bronson or Eastwood. I liked the movies and thought I was seducing him but he wound up seducing me.

"At his unit I met a retiring sergeant who wanted to finish college and go to law school. The first soldier I meet in my thirty two years of service who wants to be a lawyer—which desire he just happens to slip to this visitor!

"And did they talk! They sensed that I also didn't fit in and tried to win me over. They had friends who were killed through bureaucratic screw-ups in Grenada and Iran and were afraid that they would be next. We all knew that stupidity kills more than the enemy during wartime.

"And we *were* comrades: loving the Army and believing that the United States was the hope of the world, though maybe its ideals can only flourish here, in this very special land.

"So I came on their side. Maybe because I was getting old and had never committed myself to anything. I even promised to take his cat if he was killed, and I hate cats.

"I already knew their stories. OPERATION URGENT FURY. The nineteen eighty three invasion of Grenada after its leftist prime minister was executed by a more revolutionary deputy and Washington worried he would try to spread Communism like Cuba did.

"What really drove them crazy was how it was done. Like a public relations exercise where what was important was being part of the expected quick victory. Remember, it was called *URGENT* FURY. But the maps were out-of-date and the planners came from the Atlantic Command which was geared toward Europe, not Key West Caribbean.

"Every branch wanted their photo taken with the six hundred medical students being rescued. That no one knew where they were was the least of the military's problems.

"The Marines, 82nd Airborne, and SOF went after the same targets. Some soldiers drowned during parachute jumps because there wasn't time for a buoyancy test. Or they arrived late so there was no surprise; and had the wrong objectives, like freeing unknown political prisoners. Every essential—intelligence, planning, rehearsal—was missing. A hundred seventy were killed, more than half accidentally. Twenty percent were SOF."

Harold sipped his coffee.

"Then came DESERT ONE: the SOF attempt to rescue the embassy staff which was being kept hostage by Iran. With the same results: poor equipment and planning leading to more deaths!

"To end my story and then I'll get going. Next morning, while driving back, something The Colonel said clicked. That he appreciated my support but he didn't believe that any officer could help. Which was correct.

"What they needed was a highly placed *civilian* in the Defense Department. But not just any, for he'd be eaten alive with the Department's usual delaying-to-the-death tactics. Saying that he was trying to get the country into another Vietnam, and not returning his calls.

"So I suggested that we, note I said *we*, have as point man a civilian, to head an advisory group of *retired* officers with impeccable credentials. Who would be more likely to take a stand than active duty people. And to have this committee report to the Secretary of Defense in order to protect them, and apply pressure from above.

"We did our best and by the time I retired the Special Operations Command was running. Though it took legislation to bring it about and there are still yearly battles against it. For my retirement party SOF created a huge 'THANK YOU' sign which they later blew up. I appreciated that gesture."

Harold paused again.

"How would you like an old cat?"

"No, thanks."

"The Colonel died this morning. Suicide. He had AIDS. Who would have suspected."

I spoke cautiously, not wanting to seem insensitive but being puzzled by his depth of distress. Sadness I would expect, and the death of any relatively young person is tragic. But why did he need me—*now*.

"Were you *good* friends?"

"It wasn't like that. Not every single old guy is gay," he replied with a slight smile. I wondered how many had mistakenly concluded that about him in the course of his career.

"I'm not so dumb a psychiatrist to think it. How often did you speak with him?"

"Not since last year."

I paused for a moment. "When a person wants an immediate appointment they're very upset about something. But a week ago you said that no soldier is a stranger to death."

Another pause, now for so long that I wondered if he would speak again. Still, I was only pretending to care, being too worn down by my own fears, and hungering to cling to Gerri and temporarily forget them.

"Maybe the thoughts which his death aroused," I suggested.

"Vincent Foster."

"What about him?"

"Both suicides by pistol shot to the head. I never considered the Colonel to be gay and his girl friend is sure that he wasn't. So *was* it AIDS? Or is this intended to be a satisfying explanation, like Foster's alleged depression. Is it logical for so successful a person to kill themselves?"

No, I thought, but it was understandable. Someone at the height of his career experiences great stress, is viciously attacked and views himself as being unable to defend his friend, the president. Then, feeling deeply inadequate for the first time, he concludes himself to be unworthy of life.

But my explanation of how suicide could seem reasonable to a troubled person wasn't necessary.

"I understand how someone could kill themselves," he said. "A kid gets picked on—is too fat or whatever. The sergeant doesn't notice or ignores it, the recruit snaps, and I'm asked to investigate a suicide or murder or both.

180

"But why *his* death? Was it really AIDS—or something from his past? I might find out having been appointed executor of his estate, such as it is. That's what happens when you get old: it becomes a contest with the first one dying being the winner and the next getting all of the work."

I smiled, his bad joke being no worse than many of mine.

"So...was he deeply in the closet? Or did he know too much and was safe only in the military where they take most seriously the murder of SOF officers. But he's been retired for five years. What could he know that would threaten someone now? Questions without answers."

Like my life, I thought.

"Except for one," he quickly added. "That he had a powerful enemy. Things like this—an officer's murder, *and* your far-reaching investigation—demand that they exist."

Now Harold appeared more relaxed and confident than since his treatment began.

"I didn't know what to do an hour ago but I do now. I'm ending my retirement to find out what happened. Then we'll have a little ceremony for me and his men at his grave. Maybe a preacher too though he wasn't a believer. It's for us, not him. They'd like that. They never leave anyone behind...to be alone.

"If it wasn't suicide, someone must be punished. He was a good man and he loved his men and this country. I still have my files and credit for favors. And, The Good Lord willing, time enough to lay his ghost to rest before becoming one."

As Harold spoke, his eyes, though teary, shone, and seemed to reflect all the honor and faith of which soldiers are capable, and on which depends the ability to maintain a democracy.

He seemed finished so, after a few moments, I said my usual "we're going to have to stop now," and accepted his rib about being too predictable. Then I did my customary end-of-day tasks: straightening the chairs, emptying wastebaskets, refilling the bathroom soap dispenser.

Comforted by this routine, I viewed the office for, likely, one of my last times and noticed that Benjamin, my stuffed bear friend, had nearly fallen from the chair on which he and our other friends, Darius Dog and Burton Bird had rested. On the "snooze pillow" which his mother made for him so he had only happy dreams. I wished that someone would make me one though I wouldn't have believed in it. Just wanted to.

CHAPTER THIRTY ONE

I braved my modern gauntlet in a taxi, being thankful that the imposing traffic in the city in which I lived made chase by paparazzi improbable. And what kind of a photo would they catch anyway? Just that of a slumped down, middle aged man going home.

Arriving at the apartment house meant confronting the intense look of the now familiar reporters. They faced the confident image favored by accused mobsters and this doctor.

While in the elevator I wondered if the kids had seen me on TV and dreaded the moment when I had to confirm, what? That their stepfather was considered a murderer by prosecutors across America? That long buried bodies were being dug up for autopsy? Or maybe that I wouldn't be around much longer?

It was the last which bothered me most though I would never say any of them. Just tell them that "grown-ups sometimes say silly things," though I was sure that even three and five year olds wouldn't buy it. I never would have.

But the girls were long asleep, and had missed my "kissing them good night." Which, even if untrue, was a nice thing for Gerri to say. I was even less trusting now.

Soon we were eating and drinking the wine which she insisted on since my release from jail. In the past I rarely drank when I lived with a woman, being afraid of what I might reveal.

"How did today go?" Gerri asked.

"Clinically very good. My patients are getting it together. It's their doctor who is falling apart."

I felt that she didn't know what to say. So I did what I usually do when the silence with a patient becomes oppressive: I asked a question.

"Did the kids ask anything?"

"About what?"

Today seemed to be my day to be the butt of other people's bad jokes.

"Oh, the weather. Or how soon before Lew kills their mother!"

Gerri hugged me, this causing the wine to spill.

"Watch the blood stain," I cautioned. My jokes were deteriorating too.

We both gave up and went to bed, where she tried comforting me in the only remaining way—which didn't work since I wasn't feeling sexual. Then I remembered Joan's statement that a murder accusation focuses the mind and tried to refocus mine by helping Gerri sexually. But she also wasn't in the mood. Still, our efforts meant that we still both cared, or were trying to.

Things seemed better in the morning. My gloom was gone and I tried expanding my good mood by viewing my experience within the framework of a common event like divorce. Both involve lawyers and, sometimes, publicity, though the similarities aren't that great.

Breakfast with the kids was silliness, pancakes, and Gerri's argument with Kirsten who was developing her own style of dress. When she left, I asked who was winning. "I'm not sure," Gerri said. "It's hard to speak logically with an illogical child."

I ate two more pancakes before becoming obsessed my usual pre-arrest worry of being overweight. I considered this another indication of my healthier adjustment—until Joan called. It was seven fifteen and I thought that no non-lottery-playing person gets good news so early. It wasn't.

"We'd better talk," Joan said. "The DNA results are in."

"How? I never gave a skin sample."

"You did during some military experiment."

I vaguely remembered volunteering, this having been the only way I could get a weekend pass to meet a woman—who, with my present string of luck, I might soon be accused of murdering too.

"So?"

"Let's meet. At eight-thirty but not in my office: I don't want reporters seeing us together this early. There's a coffee-shop at two thirty one Broadway, two blocks up from City Hall. *Claude's* on the northwest corner. We'll talk then." She hung up with her not most friendly manner.

"What did she say?" Gerri asked.

"She wants to talk. I have to get going."

CHAPTER THIRTY TWO

JOAN SAT FACING front in the last booth. The restaurant seemed too crowded for a confidential lawyer/client conference since all the other tables were filled.

"They're politicians," she explained. "Coming here because it's close to their offices and the only place left which bakes their own Danish and where waiters still talk to customers. Definitely not a McDonalds."

"I can't imagine a politician taking a meet there," I said, feigning a casual tone as my stomach began rumbling. "But maybe, if New York keeps on its Midwest kick."

Joan abruptly stopped speaking, as if she wanted to weigh her words.

"I'm your lawyer and no court can demand that I reveal what you tell me. Do you really understand that?"

"Completely. Even if I confess to you, you may as well be dead."

I quickly apologized for my edged tone.

"I'm sorry. I was starting to relax and my anxiety went through the roof again when you called. Being accused of murder isn't common for any doctor."

Now Joan became nurturing and calm. I first learned that nurturing calms women from my girlfriends. My mother, who was a physician, nurtured only her patients.

"I'm sorry too. Your case is still young. I learned something and got nervous. Are you *sure* that you want me for your lawyer?"

I thought that if Joan was raising this issue again then the news must be truly awful.

"You're good for me," I said quickly. "You're bright and aggressive, and though you say you're inexperienced I'd sooner have a lawyer who admits it than one repeating thirty years of bad habits. Mine isn't the typical case where problems are plugged in and solutions pop out. I'll tell you when I don't want you. What did you learn?"

"There's a match between your DNA and that on some things in Louise's room. The D.A. is leaning towards the death penalty. A first for him."

"My parents always insisted that I be first in whatever I did," I said, mixing reality with another bad joke before becoming factual.

"How was the lab work done so quickly?"

"The FBI needs good public relations and pulled out all the stops. Your case is a godsend—their lab has come under fire."

"Deservedly so."

"Maybe, but the average juror didn't read the *Wall Street Journal's* criticism of it. To them the FBI is still the best in scientific crime busting and if they say that there's a DNA match then the accused is guilty."

"What are my options?"

"You've done forensics. An insanity defense wouldn't work. A guilty plea might save your life here though I wouldn't bet on it in Alabama. But maybe if you told everything: the names and locations of the victims, described their final minutes, things like that."

I was amazed at how calmly Joan spoke to a man she considered a multiple murderer though I knew how effective legal training could be in causing lawyers to make abstractions of people. Witnessing *their* execution is then easier.

I selected my words carefully.

"This isn't why I hired you."

"What do you mean?"

"If I wanted a typical lawyer in this era of settle, settle, settle, I wouldn't have chosen you. But I thought that you were a swashbuckler: still the Irish fighter with grandparents who clawed their way out of poverty. They called you an old woman when you started law school but you didn't let it stop you and there are probably many who still condemn you for having had a child on your own though she's a delight. You never asked me but I'm telling you that I'm innocent—no matter what any prosecutor thinks.

"We're not pleading 'guilty but insane,' which I agree no jury would believe. We're pleading 'not guilty.' And even if they decide to stick a needle in my arm or pull the switch, I want you screaming it. While wearing your purple panties!"

I thought that my last line might have gone too far but I knew that I had to lift her depression somehow, even by affirming our sexual attraction. If she felt as depressed as me, my defense was hopeless.

But I also knew that while I could be lucky enough to beat one case it was impossible for me to beat them all. So I didn't plan to stay around for my trial. I would miss Gerri and the kids: they were the closest relationship I ever had.

My monologue worked, Joan smiled, and I wondered if my leg was touching hers or the table's.

"I noticed your leer but my panties are dark red not purple."

Now I smiled. "An understandable error." Then I became serious. "How much do you know about DNA?"

"Just that when there's a match the person was definitely there—like with fingerprints."

"Let me explain. The similarities between DNA and fingerprints aren't big ones and the way the FBI uses DNA is questionable. Possibly, someday, it will be regarded as another of their disasters. Do you know the kind of DNA test they used?"

"No."

"It's crucial to find out. There are two DNA tests and one isn't very good. *Nuclear DNA* must have cell nuclei present. *Mitochondrial DNA* is more plentiful and so poorer fragments can be used. Which sounds good except that this sequence is shared by relatives, and four out of a hundred are identical. With *Nuclear DNA* the probability is one out of billions so it is much more conclusive.

"Most tests compare a small part of the DNA: that which is normally different in people. But the real odds depend on race and ethnicity since some groups are more interbred than others.

"So the test which the FBI insists is like fingerprints really isn't, though for most people DNA means *DNA fingerprints.*"

The nervous twitch on Joan's face stopped. I finished my cheese Danish, sprawled in the booth and, again, felt Joan's or the table's leg touching mine.

"Let me do the worrying. You be the doctor which is what we must emphasize to the media. That a psychiatrist's reputation has been devastated by false accusations. How about having a picture spread of your office in the *Daily News?* Not of you with patients, but the toys and stuffed animals."

"How do you know what's in my office?"

"My daughter was in therapy. She was impossible for awhile."

I weighed the pros and cons of her suggestion. A public relations campaign would make me better known but it would also cause other D.A.s to to rummage through old cases. But doctors have a reservoir of sympathy and few would believe that one could be a murderer, even if I knew differently.

I told Joan of my concern.

"It might *slow* the prosecutors and save your life," she advised.

"Or make them redouble their efforts."

"That could be."

We decided on a tailored public relations campaign: interviews by friendly reporters and a sympathetic talk-show host like Larry King. With all of them, I would discuss children's mental health issues but not my legal problems. I opposed the "at home" segment which she suggested. This would send Gerri up the wall, and me packing.

Now, both feeling relaxed and with the restaurant emptying, we ordered more coffee.

"How's your love life?" I asked. This wasn't a typical client/lawyer question but we were old acquaintances. And this question would strengthen her belief in the possibility of our eventual affair and cause her to work harder.

"*What* love life? Guys think that women lawyers are too aggressive. *City Lawyer* even stopped their personal ads—*no one* wants to date us!"

"It's the same with psychiatrists. Women are afraid that you'll analyze them. Even I never liked to date someone who was in therapy. I always behaved cautiously when I was with them." Then I quickly added, "about what I said."

"Did Gerri have therapy?"

"A little when she was a kid. Her family seems as crazy as mine, complete with a super rich relative. She also has a dead cheating husband—in a car accident."

I fantasized that if the public came to believe that Gerri had killed her husband we would become the most famous couple in the world, getting a blaring headline even in *The Economist*.

"I always wondered why you worked where you did. Yale psychiatrists aren't in rural clinics. They're in big cities making tons of money and the only Black kid they see is their doorman's. But you've treated everyone: Black, Indian, Hispanic—for peanuts or even for free. *And for years.*

"I can see why the D.A. is puzzled. You're too good for what you do so he's convinced that another motive is driving you: like the need to kill women. Or maybe Louise learned something and you had to silence her."

"You make my being a murderer sound plausible."

"That's how the DA could see it—not me."

"It looks like I need good PR."

"That's next."

"But can we keep the reporters in bounds? Stop them from wrecking what life I have left."

"We can set ground rules but reporters push and if you tell them what you shouldn't then that's your problem. Serial killers are big news. People want information to help them feel safe. But once your case is over, so will the publicity."

"I wish that I felt as optimistic."

"Remember what I said: 'I'll tell you when to worry.'"

I was grateful for Joan's support but I had no belief that I would be found innocent. I knew that most serial killers were caught by chance and not investigation. My depression returned as we left the restaurant, to go our separate ways.

CHAPTER THIRTY THREE

THE FOLLOWING DAYS went slowly as my novel routine took hold. No longer was I an anonymous resident of America's greatest city. Now my picture was in every newspaper and interviewers clamored for my attention.

If I had acting talent, I thought, this might be the start of a new career. Though I knew that I had been pretending all my life: first, in keeping my feelings secret from my parents; then, the mother's death from colleagues. Only once was I open—to a child dying from leukemia. How could I refuse her questions? Who would she tell?

Each morning I left Gerri to greet (now by name) the waiting reporters, and then took a taxi to my office. Some patients did end their treatment. Thankfully, those I was most involved with, Rev. Cary and The General, stayed. Though the reason for their torments remained unclear, as did mine.

Gerri and I grew closer. We often spoke, after the kids were sleep, of my childhood with two successful parents whose only concern was their child's academic achievements. Which did occur, though it didn't turn out as anyone expected.

Seeking to escape my father's fascination with death, I rejected his career choice of pathology and became a child psychiatrist. But his morbid preoccupation won out in the end as my life became pervaded by my recurring execution nightmare—and current murder indictment.

"The past is gone," patients would say, and I'd agree. Before adding that it influenced us through our memories. No one could escape this, I insisted, feeling certain that I never would.

Sometimes Gerri did reveal more of her life: her late husband's drinking; the beatings she received when she opposed his spanking their children; and how she got the slight break in her nose I found so attractive—and letter "S" for "Siggie" burned into her buttock.

I wasn't surprised for I knew how much women would bear to protect their children. Now I understood her murderous rage towards him. Still, she was usually reflective, like the archetypal Midwest woman I always sought. My mother was quiet too, but cold.

"Would you mind if a relative visited?" Gerri asked. "He'll stay at a hotel. Even if we had the room he's very private."

"I'd be glad to speak about normal things with anyone but am probably news in Denmark too. Maybe you have your own headline: HOMETOWN GIRL MAKES GOOD?"

As Gerri grabbed for my hair, I sensed that we were exploring a new type of love, one which neither of us had been free enough to experience earlier. Maybe, I hoped, life will grant a second chance. Then I started crying as I never did when I was a child: why should I cry when there was no one to hear me?

"Who's coming?" I asked.

"Maurice...Kirsten's godfather."

"Is he related?"

"Not by blood. He's in his seventies and knew my family for years. His family was murdered by the Nazis so work became his life: buying ships, factories, newspapers. Just by glancing at a company's books he can see how it can be restructured. He buys companies cheaply and holds on.

"After what he went through not many people can be completely normal. He was married four times and after each divorce he set up a new household with his wife and ex-wives and children. You'll like him—you're both very bright."

I'd love to speak with anyone, I thought, who didn't treat me as the media monster I had become. So I looked forward to Maurice's visit as did the girls, though for them he was the exotic relative who sent expensive presents.

Despite Gerri's comment I didn't think that we were similar even with my enormously wealthy grandfather. None of whose dollars trickled down to my mother for he had resented her accomplishments. But he was good to me, though never speaking of his life. Every family is so filled with secrets, I thought. Which, being a psychiatrist, I knew shouldn't surprise me.

Thus my trial approached. I initially planned to flee and disappear again into backwoods America. Maybe had I stayed there my problems never would have happened. Another maybe, even as I knew that I couldn't avoid the influence of my past.

It was Gerri and the kids which kept me here. Those invisible strands which bind people were strengthening and each day I became less able to view my life living alone. Though telling myself that I should leave and allow them to get on with normal lives. Maybe, someday, I could return and view them from afar. More maybes.

But how could I treat them like this? Gerri's beauty *would* attract another man. But I remembered what Karen said of her father's death, "It broke me and mommy's heart." As would happen again if I fled.

While deciding, I continued accumulating cash and investigating rural destinations. Possibly I would wind up committing suicide like so many fugitives. But is this worse than dying at some state's hand? At least I would be controlling my dismal fate, thinking in my last moments of Gerri and what might have been. And with my parents and grandfather too. Then I cried again.

CHAPTER THIRTY FOUR

THE STATE BEGAN investigating my fitness to practice medicine. While no patient had filed a complaint, the vaguely written regulations enabled a doctor to lose his license for whatever reason the Board considered sufficient. A new problem for me.

The only good news was that no further evidence was found which linked me to Louise's death. A witness remembered a tall figure leaving the building on the night of her murder. But they wore a raincoat and were viewed from a distance. Yet the DNA findings, Louise's note, diary, comment to her friend, and the blood and hair spattered walking stick seemed evidence enough. There was no mention of a plea bargain, which I wouldn't have accepted anyway since it wouldn't protect me from the other state's prosecutors.

Who were digging. Periodically, deteriorated body parts would be found but the resultant lust to associate me with them remained unsatisfied. As new ones were discovered, my picture and story again blared about the globe, disappearing when no additional details surfaced.

How did I manage to survive? By involving myself with Gerri, the kids, and, particularly, my work. Work binds one to reality, Freud wrote. But it also protected me from the pain I faced and gave me perspective. As did my new interest in religion.

I last attended synagogue as a teenager, dutifully following my mother who became a power in whatever she did, even as convert to Judaism. My later rejection of religion derived from my rejecting my parents' values for nothing is more basic to parents than their religion. So I became like the policeman's child who steals or the teacher's child who fails. But I would never have been arrested or failed—not with *my* parents.

Later, as a psychiatrist, I enjoyed helping clergy cope with the tension between their personal needs and their professional demands. It was comforting to view existence within the framework of thousands of years of people trying to understand their destiny by creating and following religious beliefs.

The same peace which I felt at my parents' funeral after their plane crashed while enroute to a conference on (of all things) the ethics in transplant procedures. It held little interest for them but they loved Charleston and thus had died for a tax deductible perk...

Their service were held in the synagogue to which my parents belonged. One mourner described a prank I had long forgotten: my dropping of water filled balloons from its roof. They were really condoms from my mother's desk but I didn't correct him—too many people already believe that psychiatrists are weird!

As the rabbi described my parents' virtues, I suddenly realized that they *were* loved, even if not by their son. Why did I not love them, I wondered. Did they love me? I had felt only anger towards them. But I did cry, for the first time, at their funeral. As do most children, however inadequate their parents were.

Surprisingly, my grandfather did come, arriving in an old, chauffeur driven Lincoln limousine. He hadn't attended his daughter's wedding and this was likely the first time that he was in a synagogue. But he dutifully put on the black skullcap which was handed him and which went well with his black suit. It was double breasted and, like his automobile, memorialized a long past era, and I wondered at his perspective on his long life. His daughters regarded him as a monster but, always having been solitary, I too felt alienated from normal experiences and empathized with him.

So we embraced as we had when I was a child, and I hoped that he would tell me of his life as my parents rarely did of theirs.

All my aunts who weren't in a psychiatric hospital were there. But they spoke little and seemed uncomfortable. It was likely that they attended only at their father's insistence for they always did everything he wanted.

CHAPTER THIRTY FIVE

W**HILE AWAITING TRIAL**, my life became almost normal. I was as silly as ever with the kids and we made pancakes, which I had difficulty eating now that my electrocution nightmare had returned.

All spoke excitedly of Maurice's visit. "He'll bring you something too," Gerri told me, "he likes buying people things." So I awaited my gift, feeling continually groggy from the lack of sleep which my napping only partly remedied. I felt bound to my present but also detached from it and wondered how soon before trial I would flee.

I felt like I had one foot in New York City and the other...? I didn't yet know. Somewhere I could work using false identification, though not as a physician. Even as fugitive I recoiled from using another's medical credentials.

Yet during these troubled days I felt closer to everyone—Gerri and the kids, my patients, Joan—than before. Savoring each remaining moment, I anticipated leaving the City as I had once returned, with only cash and the stuffed animals who long since developed their own personalities. We were all good friends as they shared their idealized fifties' family life with me.

My depression finally lifted as I realized that I truly loved Gerri, the kids, and my work. And, despite how my life turned out, I had lived as I was compelled to. I could have made better choices but didn't and, realizing this, I forgave myself.

Now something Cary said struck a chord. That he had never understood the Christian philosophy of hating the sin but not the sinner for how could one hate evil but not the person doing it? Then he realized that he could love himself even if hating some of the things which he did, and he became convinced that whatever is sought with faith will be received.

So I prayed. Having lived my life driven by unknown motives, what harm could prayer do?

Unsure how, I fantasized being known to a godlike figure and, admittedly an unusual act for a psychiatrist, offered myself to view. For long minutes there was...nothing. Then, suddenly, I no longer felt alone but as I had at my parents' funeral: buoyed by the sense of another standing by me and a tradition spanning a hundred generations.

I now concluded that, in their own way, my parents loved had me, and that all children are lovable even if not believing so. A popular thought which I told to countless others but had never applied to myself.

And as my life drew to a close, for even if I fled I expected that it would soon end, I felt a sense of harmony. I knew that I had tried to live an honorable life and would live an honorable death. And that because of my work many people were healed, and I would live on in their memories. Now I finally felt a sense of peace, and my execution nightmare no longer occurred.

CHAPTER THIRTY SIX

Our public relations campaign began. A reporter/photographer invaded my office and expressed surprise that it lacked an analyst's couch, though this was absent from most practices for a generation. Despite my anxiety, I told well-disguised stories and offered parenting suggestions. She seemed impressed, but I was always a clever, amusing speaker.

Her story contained little about my "legal problems" (to put it mildly) and contained mostly my comparison of city and rural youth, who weren't so different at all.

Joan complimented me on the story and negotiated ground-rules for my TV appearance. Gerri liked it, and more tenants began riding with me in the elevator again. While I didn't believe these events to have religious significance, Cary might have disagreed.

He insisted that affliction is the only way to become fully alive and, rather than disproving the existence of a loving deity, exemplified His presence. Without it, God would be dead. Then, out of the blue, he quoted a sixteenth century clergyman, George Herbert: "Love bade me welcome but my soul drew back."

I felt stunned and immediately thought that these words explained my execution nightmare: that rejecting love would lead to death. It sounded good but didn't ring true. Cary's statement interrupted my musing about myself.

"You can speak to my wife if you want."

"Are you sure? You had objected to it."

"It'll be OK. What will you tell her about me?"

"Just what's in *both* your interests. But I'll need your written consent. Don't sign the form if you're committed to getting divorced for then everything could wind up in court."

"No. We believe in Christ's words that a man and wife are of 'one flesh' and divorce the cutting of a living body. She's given me something which I've never had in another relationship: the continuous impact of something close and real."

⊠⊠⊠⊠⊠⊠⊠

My daytime life continued. I now spent more evenings helping Joan for it was difficult to find friendly experts even for the stiff fee which we offered. She was leery of my testifying, believing that this would open me to questions about the woman's death in Chicago and prejudice the jury. As would information about my past numerous affairs and what these angry women might still say.

I felt strongly that the DNA evidence could be shaken but not the rest of it, and particularly Louise's comment to her roommate about our scheduled meeting.

Joan tried to reassure me by describing John Peel's *two* murder trials in Alaska—despite there being no motive or witness tying him to the crime. The first jury favored acquittal; the second attended his celebration. But her attempt backfired.

"The D.A. *does have* reasonable evidence and motive."

She became silent though just briefly, not wanting me to get depressed again.

"The cases aren't exactly alike," she agreed. "My point is that you shouldn't be discouraged. Jurors are independent no matter what a prosecutor insists, and I'll be with you all the way!" As I knew that she would.

The General canceled his weekly appointment, saying that he was flying to Washington to meet with old friends, but not whether it concerned The Colonel's death.

My life seemed awash in dead bodies. In the past I resented energetic play therapy with children but now welcomed this diversion, knowing that after they shot me with a toy gun I was still alive.

CHAPTER THIRTY SEVEN

Cary's wife, Jane, awaited me at the door of my office. I had expected her to be frantic and disheveled like the other troubled wives I treated but was wrong.

She was prettier than I imagined for a clergyman's wife, with glossy black hair and flawless skin. Dressed in a gray jacket, off-white sweater, and gray patterned skirt, with a single strand of pearls and thin wedding band. While not Armani, her clothes were more Lord and Taylor than Banana Republic. Distinctions I became capable of making after two weeks of living with Gerri. I wondered if the pearls were real and whether she worked, having mistakenly assumed that she was the archetypal fifties' housewife as I had become the nineties' serial killer.

Unlike her husband, she immediately accepted coffee.

"Cary signed a form which lets me share information and I ask that you do the same. It frees me to explain matters to you both."

"Fine," she said. As I handed her the paper I noticed that she wore the same perfume as Gerri, an old Chanel, and felt momentarily disconcerted.

"How are things between you?" I asked.

"Not good. He's preoccupied and moody though less so since seeing you. He's not a good manager. He demands my help but then resents my doing the church's books. I'd be a CPA if he let me get the work experience which I need for the exam."

"Why won't he?"

"He says that my job is to help him. Forty years ago that would have been acceptable, but today wives lead separate lives. They'd think better of him the more money I made. It impresses even churchgoers."

"What do they know about his difficulties?"

"Some probably suspect that something is up. The woman complained to the bishop who held a closed investigation. She doesn't plan to sue but maybe she will change her mind so it's good that I have a profession to support us."

"How much do you know about the complaint?"

"Bits. She felt uncomfortable having the door closed... he implied having sex with her and others."

"How did you feel when you found out?"

"Angry...frustrated."

"How so?"

"Cary's warm, bright, even funny—with others. And definitely good looking. Like a filled-out Jimmy Stewart, whose movies he shows to illustrate painful dilemmas. I can understand women falling in love with him—I did.

"But he's too independent for most churches. He's unwilling to compromise and when members object he tends to create a crisis which *forces him* to reconsider and to accept what he had earlier rejected as being a betrayal of his principles."

"Do you plan to stay with him?"

She seemed surprised by my question.

"*Always*, though sometimes I want to kill him. He's missing something in the way he relates. He says things that drive people up the wall and then wonders why they scheme against him. I can imagine what he might have told you when he began therapy: he can be nasty when he's frightened."

"What does he tell you?"

"The usual: that I'm a controlling bitch and don't deserve a love like his, which no other man would give me. Then he wonders why I put up with him and apologizes no end. St. John said 'if our heart condemns us, God is greater than our heart.' I don't know why he feels so guilty. He *should* for the dumb things he says but it's something else and I don't have a clue. Maybe you can find out."

"What were his parents like?"

"His father was a college engineering teacher. Popular on campus but a deadly bore at home. His mother was just lethal. He set fires as a kid: small ones, no one was hurt. And he secretly sucked his thumb until he was seventeen. I know because we were friends since the first grade, so maybe we both need therapy."

I changed the subject. Cary's church wasn't paying for *her* treatment.

"Did you feel betrayed when you heard about his affair with the parishioner?"

She smiled wearily. "He's fooled you too."

"How do you mean?" I asked, but sensed what she was about to reveal.

"There was no sex no matter what he implied. If he touched her it couldn't have been more than patting her shoulder. The rest is her imagination. She said she felt *uncomfortable*. How many women feel that with their doctor? He barely touches me."

"How often do you have sex?"

"When he doesn't 'have a headache' or isn't 'tired' or 'have a sermon to write.' Four times a year though he sure exudes sex appeal. There *were* no affairs. He loses erections and I'm the only woman he would trust to know this. I don't know how this and his Jimmy Stewart pretension fit together but maybe Jimmy had them too."

"It's called 'splitting,'" I said. "The mind's ability to separate conflicting information in order to be able to keep a desired self-image. One minute a person relates to one aspect of themselves, the next to another. Each is 'split-off,' and they don't come together."

"How long can it last?"

"Maybe all one's life."

"What can I do? I'm tired of supporting him through crises."

"Encourage him to stay in therapy. Patients resent feeling that they have to answer for their behavior, which isn't what happens there. A good therapist almost never gives advice—they can get that from their bartender. I make suggestions which I ask be considered but only if they want to. I'm not God." Then I smiled and added, "But I do help out when He's on vacation."

She nodded, recognizing my attempt to lighten our discussion. We both knew that it wasn't easy for her to speak openly. Facts are often unwelcome—like the burned "S" on Gerri's buttock.

I had never asked her about it, not wanting to know the details even as I touched the scarified tissue. No wonder she stayed with me: murder indictment or not, I was great compared with her dead husband, Siggie!

What kind of woman would permit herself to be burned. Was she drunk? Or, despite her impressive, self-assured appearance, was she partly still the girl who had tried to kill herself at thirteen. Then came an adolescent affair, a long period of celibacy, marriage to Siggie, and finally me. A puzzling life.

And what of Cary's allusions to extramarital intimacies and his wife's aversion to sex? All were lies to conceal his distress at being impotent, and...?

Once he quoted Blake's poem of Christ's birth, "My mother groaned, my father wept. Into the dangerous world I leapt." So, when not confronting real peril as in Vietnam, Cary hatched crises. And what greater calamity for a clergyman than to be accused of betraying his congregation. Then having to seek atonement, following undeserved punishment.

I wondered how much the bishop knew. Being psychologically sophisticated, he always refused to discuss his clergy's personal psychological problems, saying that they were my business. But if he took the parishioner's charge seriously he would have suspended Cary.

No, Cary's real danger lay within himself. I wondered what other fantasies propped up his life...and Gerri's...and mine...

This session was a good one. As Jane passed me while leaving, I again noticed Gerri's scent and suddenly realized why she had accepted abuse despite her high intelligence.

There are traits associated with masculinity and femininity. A man is expected to be assertive and a woman to express concern. So were Gerri not "understanding" of Siggie's rage she would have betrayed her identity. I wondered again about her sexual passivity. So like my long past girlfriend who first had sex at twelve...with her father...

CHAPTER THIRTY EIGHT

My TRIAL ARRIVED. The squirreled away money and vague plans were ready but I had not left, feeling that I spent my life fleeing and now had nowhere to go. Maybe if Gerri agreed to accompany me I would be already gone. But this was such madness that I never suggested it. Though she might have agreed. She just might have agreed...

Gerri took the kids to day-care early on the first day of my trial. Then we held each other. We were now sure that we would be together until the end.

And I did what I had not done in twenty years and which symbolized how much my life had changed: turned off my pager. Thus violating my fervent belief that a doctor should *always* be available to their patients. I wanted to turn off the phone too but Gerri feared that the children might need her. As she spoke, I noticed acne on her forehead. Some doctors still deny that stress affects the skin but no woman I treated ever believed them.

We dressed slowly. I, in a sober black suit; she, in the simple black dress which Joan suggested. Then we sat silently until eight, one and a half hours before my trial began. I knew that we would be early and likely arrive even before the reporters. I was always afraid to be late though I expected, soon, for others to take on this responsibility for me.

Gerri went to get the elevator. As I locked the door, the phone rang but it was too late. My future, *our* future, awaited us downtown.

Surprisingly, there were no reporters at our building's entrance so, rather than get a taxi, we took the subway which is much faster during rush hour.

There, reporters milled about the courthouse and, upon seeing us, they surged in our direction though it was Joan who reached us first. She had a broad smile on her face. A weird look, I felt, for what I faced.

"It's all over," she said, "The D.A. is dropping the charges."

Though I cried only once until recently, I was always afraid of crying in public but I didn't now. Gerri cried. I fainted.

CHAPTER THIRTY NINE

THIS WAS TO be the end of the memoir which I began writing after Joan advised of our need to better understand my crisis. Which is now over though precisely why may never be known. So I didn't plan to write more until The General phoned to schedule an appointment. "It's dangerous keeping a diary but sometimes worse not having one," he said.

Thus my writing continues.

I fainted momentarily but my vision returned as my body hit the ground. The photograph favored by tabloids showed my head in Gerri's lap with tears flowing down her cheeks. I closed my eyes—the TV lights were blinding—but was helped to my feet and quickly bundled into Joan's car after I refused medical attention.

I didn't know why the case was dropped. Cary once quoted Mark that a prayer made with extraordinary faith will be answered. But followed with James' qualification, that it could be refused.

I didn't pray for this improbable outcome—only that Gerri remain with me. Realistically, what more could I have hoped?

Gerri insisted that I lie down while Joan explained.

"The *Daily News* received a photo of Louise holding a newspaper which was sent by FedEx from Watertown, South Dakota. Along with her fingerprints, and a note saying that you'll always be her doctor. The package arrived early this morning and they notified the court.

"Without a motive you can't be tied to the body they found. The D.A. now believes that Louise wanted to cause you grief but changed her mind. Your door is unlocked when you see patients. The sweater could have been taken from your closet and the walking stick from the stand. The dead woman could be someone she knew from a shelter, or a lucky find from her wanderings: a body which resembled her. But why did she go to *South Dakota*?"

I knew why. While treating Louise I often described the friendlier atmosphere of rural America, and now wondered what identity she adopted. As grieving widow? Unemployed divorcee? She loved practicing the artful resumes I created. Thankfully, her package was sent by Fed-Ex. Were it mailed, the first morning of my trial would now be ending.

An elderly psychiatrist once told me that troubled people can draw you into their problems. Yet though Louise forced me to recognize that I would always be part of her life, I'm convinced that she never would have harmed me. But maybe I was wrong about her, like I was with Cary.

"What about the other states prosecuting me?"

"They never found anything tying you to a body. They just jumped on the best possibility in years of closing old cases to relieve public anxiety. Now you're an embarrassment. An *almost* miscarriage of justice which doesn't look good with the push for capital punishment. You're verging on being worth just a small paragraph under the Spelling Bee winners. It's over."

And that's what happened: I became a nobody again. Gerri wanted to celebrate but couldn't decide who to invite: those who said they *knew* I wasn't a murderer—after cold-shouldering me!

So we celebrated with just the girls. Who didn't have a clue why they could now order whatever they wanted from the Chinese restaurant's delivery menu, or stay up until midnight. Or why Lew was sillier than usual, and mommy so weepy.

CHAPTER FORTY

WELCOME, NORMAL DAYS. Gerri got a call saying that Maurice would stay at the Essex House Hotel on Central Park South. It wasn't far from my office and we planned to meet there for Saturday brunch after I finished work. He waited in its Cafe Botanica, seated at a large round table beside a chair filled with gaily wrapped packages.

Tall and spare with blond/white hair, the half-sized reading glasses perched on his nose gave him a professorial look. Gerri embraced him, I shook hands, and the girls offered theirs at her suggestion. He shook them formally.

To alleviate awkwardness, Gerri said she was hungry and that the girls had little breakfast. She suggested that we visit the buffet which held an extraordinary selection including, of course in New York City, lox.

Maurice and I had cold whitefish and black bread; Gerri, lobster. The girls chose tiny sausages, this choice arousing their mother's glare which they ignored.

We busied ourselves eating. I felt uncomfortable, having rarely related to past girlfriends' relatives, usually ending our relationship before this intimacy developed. Maurice seemed comfortable—or maybe his drinking wine helped.

"Do you ever gamble?" he asked me.

"No."

"It relaxes me."

"What do you play?"

"The western version of *pai gow* which means "heavenly dominoes" but uses cards and gives a skillful player an edge. It's slow and you can learn while playing, not losing much so long as you remain objective. How does that sound to you?"

I sensed that he was studying me, but remained mindful of Gerri's insistence that I behave with greater tact.

"I'm all for objectivity but I don't have the patience for games except for those I play with kids. I relax by being silly."

"I never had that luxury," he replied in a deprecating tone. Then, as if recognizing the harshness in his voice, he added, "until now." As he smiled, his face lost its severity and I understood why Gerri maintained contact with him.

Maurice indicated the boxes.

"Which is for Kirsten?" he asked, beaming at her. Then, noting Gerri's frown, he quickly added, "and which is for big girl Karen?"

Kirsten gushed at her new doll house which was complete with lights, an operating elevator, and elaborate furnishings.

Karen smiled politely at her antique porcelain doll. It was too expensive for play and intended for adult collectors. Unlike her sister, Karen preferred sports equipment to dolls or clothes.

The children played with their presents as Gerri and I picked at the remaining food. Then a desert cart appeared and brunch wore on.

Maurice's suggestion of a carriage ride through Central Park created glee even in the usually subdued Karen who *loved* horses. The interpretation went through my mind that such girls usually have sexual problems when they are older. But even in *my* most tactless moment I wouldn't tell Gerri this.

Maurice spoke with the concierge who talked with the doorman who flagged a carriage in a manner similar to getting a taxi. Which surprised me, having such a modern gesture be associated with so ancient a conveyance.

The girls were covered with blankets which the driver provided. Gerri held Karen, and Maurice, Kirsten. I felt uneasy riding beside autos in a fragile cart but I followed the calm horse's lead. As the carriage's rhythm soothed me, I puzzled over Maurice and why he was visiting. He was more thoughtful and indirect in speech than I expected.

Gerri had described him as being a friend who, having lost his relatives in the Holocaust, adopted her family as surrogate. All grew closer as he became wealthier though I wondered how he introduced his multiple wives. Likely such matters become unimportant as fewer years remain, I concluded.

Our ride continued. I had still kept to my Saturday nap routine and, having missed it, became drowsy. I heard Maurice murmur to Kirsten and looked sleepily at them through eyes blinded by the sun as we left a shaded roadway, I realized that they had the same facial structure —as if they were parent and child. And suddenly everything became clear: the older man whose love had saved the teenage Gerri's life. And why she now phoned Maurice so frequently—because he was also Kirsten's father.

Gerri noted my gaze, then gripped my hand as other thoughts ran through my mind: that she knew that I realized the truth, and loved us both. And, during the torment of her marriage, had sought aid from one who would never permit she or their daughter to be harmed. A man with immense wealth and shrewdness, and the contacts to insure that what had to be done was done well. So the "accident" occurred, Siggie was dead, and Gerri and Kirsten were safe.

Until Gerri met another man and Maurice, knowing of her tendency to become involved with abusive men, made inquiries and discovered that her paramour had killed a woman, and the many he dated had little good to say of him. Then Maurice again feared for Gerri's and their child's safety and acted to protect them, as he always would.

Now I wondered whether Louise was still alive, so unstable and talkative a witness as she would be. It would have been easy to learn about her: she sometimes stood outside my building and followed me. Perhaps she had presented with the possibility of achieving her dream: being able to begin a new life wherever she wanted, so long as it was far from New York.

And why had so many prosecutors considered me a killer? This belief wouldn't be difficult to arouse by someone who owned newspapers and government officials, and was used to being obeyed.

Even my tax problem disappeared. Paul, my lawyer and gifted amateur physician, described his talk with the IRS agent as being "... most productive. She offered a seventeen hundred dollar settlement, I twelve, and we split the difference and went to lunch though she wouldn't let me pay for her. Did I tell you that I helped to write the nineteen eighty six tax bill?" He didn't, but I knew why the investigator could afford the expensive lunch.

Yet *why did* Maurice change his mind and save me? Because Gerri had told him that I loved their child, or...?

Maurice distributed other gifts before leaving. Gerri's was a platinum Patek Philippe watch which showed the time simultaneously in New York and on the island they first met. Mine, a gold chain and pendant inscribed with Hebrew letters. I accepted it thankfully and began wearing it daily as he suggested, almost entreated.

A week later, as Cary was leaving my office and I held the door, my collar was open and he asked to see it. Then he asked if I knew what the words meant, and gently criticized me in a tone of mock anger and mild exasperation after my negative response.

"You know *less* about religion than my most uneducated parishioner. *Hata* is the most important word in Jewish thinking about sin. It describes a wrong action being applied to a wrong aim. But to sin is human and for humans there can always be repentance. So after one sins and misses the right road there is always *shuv*, meaning to return. One repents by journeying along the right road again."

So Maurice repented, though I wondered what repentance was adequate for three murders. Or two? Or none? Perhaps Siggie's and his girlfriend's deaths *were* accidents, Louise's alleged corpse was that of an already dead woman, and Louise still lived.

Cary, reverently, returned the pendant. Then, maybe responding to my confused look, he quoted a Talmudic saying that no person stands higher than one who has turned from the wrong path. "Not even angels," he added.

"I think the Old Testament prophet, Ezekiel, expressed this principle best of all," Cary concluded, using the instructional tone he adopted when explaining religious concepts to me. "Have I any pleasure at all that the wicked should die, says the Lord God, and not rather that he should return from his ways and live?"

Now Cary's eyes locked onto mine. "Who *should* judge another—even Judas? Perhaps God and he peered into the other. One choosing; the other chosen—and changed. To deepen His covenant with mankind."

CHAPTER FORTY ONE

Weeks passed. Kirsten "adopted" Karen's doll and spent hours playing with it. They still criticized my pancakes while gobbling them down, and Gerri's acne disappeared.

Paul called late one evening. He had begun advising doctors on financial matters and wondered if I was interested in this service. I said that I would welcome it, knowing that he would only act as advisor and not hold assets, this being an important consideration for one as distrustful as me.

Paul again spoke of the stress his teenagers were causing him, and a thought occurred to me.

"I have a middle-aged patient who has suffered from the same nightmare all his life. Maybe you can figure it out."

"I read Freud for months and always carry a paperback of one of his works. What is it?"

"He's awaiting execution, sees an electric chair or is about to, and then wakes in panic. It's the *sight* of the electric chair which terrifies him. Nothing ever happens. I don't have a clue."

"When did it start?"

"At five."

"What were his parents like?"

"Controlling and cold. They cared for him physically but that's about all."

"Think! And you call yourself a *child* psychiatrist," he said mockingly.

"How so?"

"Kids that age *must* begin to be independent of their parents. He felt that they were trying to stop this so he thought of killing them. For a young child the thought is the same as the deed. The dream symbolized his warning to himself against committing murder since he needed them to survive. He must have felt tremendous guilt all his life."

I was stunned—and wondered why I had missed this obvious interpretation.

"I'm sure that you're right. You've really helped him."

He laughed. "Maybe now your nightmare will go away."

The dream's memory remained too painful for me to join his amusement.

"Am I that clear?"

"Calm down. Probably just to me."

"I tell everyone that the best doctor I know is a tax lawyer."

He laughed again. "Next year take *all* of my advice. Maybe we can keep you out of jail."

We both laughed and I said we would have to get together for a drink though knowing that we never would.

Some friendships deteriorate during personal contact. We had never met during the eleven years I consulted him, exchanging information by fax or mail or phone.

It was seventy thirty and time for my before-leaving-the-office routine: changing wastebasket liners, checking bathroom supplies, straightening chairs. The doorbell rang and, moments later, I heard the elevator door close. On my doorstep lay a large white box sealed with thin string.

I sat on a waiting room chair, thinking that it came from Louise and being afraid to open it. Then, angry for being so fearful at my age, I carelessly cut the string with the edge of a key. Inside was an envelope and, separated by white tissue sheets, layers of anisette and almond Italian cookies. The note read:

"You should not have feared to seek my expurtise(sic). I enjoy helping people. Favors create understanding not obligation. Thank you for my daughters happiness. We hope for a boy soon.

It was signed "E."

I understood at once, knowing how important sons were in Italian families, having treated two of the seven daughters in one and wondering if their immigrant father persisted. In the past I would have been critical of Enrico's misspelling and absent apostrophe but such things no longer mattered.

He appreciated what I did for his children and knew, despite a life so different from mine, what was important: hope, children, and the faith that they would lead better lives. I would call him. This we could share, and maybe other matters too.

I was tired and longed to be home, now for the first time in my life that I had a real home.

CHAPTER FORTY TWO

"**M**ommy wants you. It's...about...*im-po-tent*."

"No, honey, the word's *im-por-tant* not *impotent*. Daddy doesn't have that problem. He just sometimes gets scared when he's feeling close to mommy."

"What?"

"I'm sorry. Daddy's being silly again. I'll talk to mommy."

Kirsten looked puzzled yet thoughtful. Regretting my impulsive words and hoping to discourage her interest in this adult matter, I pretended to ride a horse out of the room. She smiled, but I wondered what she might have overheard and remembered her past statement that she knew a lot about babies from listening to grown-ups.

Gerri was busy at her computer and said that we would talk after the kids were asleep. She was abrupt and I wondered what I could have done, or if something from her past was troubling her.

Later, grasping a rectangular package, she motioned with her other hand which held a wide glass.

"Come into the bathroom," she demanded.

Once there, she locked the door and took off her robe. She was naked. I moved to grab her but she shrugged away my hands.

"We're not here for that—read the instructions," she ordered, handing me the package. It was a pregnancy test kit. "You were there at the beginning if there was one and you'll bloody well be with me all the way. Siggie wasn't but you will!"

She squatted, peed into the glass, and handed it to me. Then she sat on the toilet and finished. I felt embarrassed.

"Don't look so uneasy. And you're even a doctor. Maybe men wouldn't be so squeamish if they had babies."

I felt like saying that I became a psychiatrist because I disliked dealing with bodily functions but she didn't look as if she would appreciate the crack. So I did as she said: put the glass on the sink and read the instructions. Then I dipped the wand into the glass with my right hand while stroking her hair with my left. As we waited the five minutes, she continued sitting, with her head bowed.

Then, in a softer tone than I ever heard, she asked, "well?" and repeated her question more softly.

I raised the wand, noted whether one or two colored lines were visible, and then dropped it back into the glass before turning towards her. Finally, she looked up.

AUTHOR'S NOTE

THIS BOOK BEGAN with my brief thought: to write of a middle aged man who, after finally achieving love, experiences great peril. It developed from there. In later volumes: Lew's family expands; The General seeks a murderer; and the Reverend Cary learns that goodness and reason are not always adequate weapons against evil.

While I had intended to begin writing of Lew's later experiences immediately after *Park West's* publication, my interest suddenly turned to another novel, *Ghosts and Angels*, which contains an even more powerful spiritual element, and to my second book on psychotherapy, *Shopping For A Shrink*. As my first literary agent, the late Harriet Pilpel, once told me, a book gets written when the writer feels that they *must* write it.

While the information in *Park West* about symptoms and psychotherapy is accurate, all characters are, of course, fictional.

Comments are, as always, welcome.

Stanley Goldstein
Hudson Valley, New York
November, 2002 – December, 2010

E-mail: drstan@*drstanleygoldstein.com*
Website: *www.drstanleygoldstein.com*

BIBLIOGRAPHY/READING SUGGESTIONS

Mark Adkin, *Urgent Fury: The Battle for Grenada* (London: Lexington Books, 1989).

Mark M. Boatner III, *Military Customs and Traditions* (Westport: Greenwood Press, 1976).

John E. Douglas and Mark Olshaker, *Journey Into Darkness: Follow the FBI's Premier Investigative Profiler as He Penetrates the Minds and Motives of the Most Terrifying Serial Killers* (New York: Scribner, 1997).

James S. Grotstein, *Splitting and Projective Identification* (Northvale: Jason Aronson, 1986). Likely difficult reading for laymen.

Harry Guntrip. "My Experience of Analysis With Fairbairn and Winnicott (How Complete a Result Does Psycho-Analytic Therapy Achieve?)," *Int. Rev. Psycho-Anal.* 2 (1975), 145-156. A personally revealing, posthumously published paper. Even if you don't understand the concepts, you'll be moved. If you have only time to read *two* from this list, choose this and one of Masterson's books. If *three*, add Kardiner's. If *four*, add Paffenroth.

Sheldon Heath, *Dealing With the Therapist's Vulnerability to Depression* (Northvale: Jason Aronson, 1991).

Phillip M. Helfaer, *The Psychology of Religious Doubt* (Boston: Beacon Press, 1972).

A. Kardiner, *My Analysis with Freud: Reminiscences* (New York: W. W. Norton, 1977).

Susan L. Marquis, *Unconventional Warfare: Rebuilding U.S. Special Operations Forces* (Washington: Brookings Institution Press, 1997).

James F. Masterson, *Treatment of the Borderline Adolescent: A Developmental Approach* (New York: Wiley, 1972). His next book is intended for layman and an easier read.

James F. Masterson, *The Search For The Real Self: Unmasking the Personality Disorder of Our Age* (New York: The Free Press, 1990).

J. Reid Meloy, ed., *The Psychology of Stalking: Clinical and Forensic Perspectives* (San Diego: Academic Press, 1998).

William Robert Miller, *Contemporary American Protestant Thought, 1900-1970* (Indianapolis: Bobbs-Merrill, 1973).

Joel Norris, *Serial Killers* (New York: Anchor Books, 1989).

Kim Paffenroth, *Judas: Images of the Lost Disciple* (Louisville: Westminster John Knox Press, 2001). A slim, thoughtful, and immensely valuable work.

Arthur Carl Piepkorn, *Profiles in Belief: the Religious Bodies of the United States and Canada* (New York: Harper & Row, 1977-1979).

Robert L. Snow, *Stopping a Stalker: A Cop's Guide to Making the System Work for You* (New York: Plenum Trade, 1998).

Bradley C. S. Watson, "The Western Ethical Tradition and the Morality of the Warrior," *Armed Forces & Society* 26 (Fall 1999): 55-72.

Joseph Wortis, *Fragments of an Analysis With Freud* (New York: Jason Aronson, 1991). Read this and Kardiner's book. Then decide which doctor you feel you would have most benefited from treatment with. My choice would be Kardiner, even considering that one can never be sure of how a patient will be treated from what the doctor wrote. Or, as Lew said, of the actual events in treatment from the patient's description of them. The most gifted child analyst I ever met regretted that he could not write.

Samuel Yochelson and Stanton E. Samenow, *The Criminal Personality, Volume II: The Change Process* (New York: Jason Aronson, 1977). A long (578 pages) but important book.

Another Great Book

Stanley Goldstein's First Novel
Lies In Progress

About *Lies In Progress*: A pregnant teenager, rejected by her parents and sought by police throughout the world, is hidden and cared for by friends. Foreseeing her murder, she prays only that her child survive and, someday, know how much she loved him. But the girl has unknown allies: a priest who delights in classical study; a congressional aide so skillful he's nicknamed "The Lord"; and an English outlaw on his final, most dangerous mission: to rescue his sister, safeguard America from the awesome weapon *CATACLYSM*—and gain redemption.

Having characters of dimension and intelligence, this novel is a moral and political odyssey of our time, destined to be shared and remembered.

FOREWORD of *Lies In Progress*

THE TV NEWS droned on as he explained my poisoning. Torn refugees and smartly dressed soldiers; then an eleven year old baton twirler whose loose costume anticipated my diminishing curves.

Later we viewed a documentary of the husband who disposed of his wife's body fragments in a stream. Hopefully she was dead before chipping began. If guidelines for lovers still exist *that* should be first!

Or is murder now acceptable with a great political career at stake? When some things must simply be done and not considered.

An E-book edition of *Lies In Progress* will be available in early 2011.

www.ingramcontent.com/pod-product-compliance
Lightning Source LLC
Chambersburg PA
CBHW030916120626
46554CB00001B/172